DAYS OF GOOD HOPE

Paul Wilson lives in Blackburn, Lancashire.
His first novel, *The Fall from Grace of Harry Angel*, was
published in 1994.

DAYS OF GOOD HOPE

Paul Wilson

JONATHAN CAPE
LONDON

First published 1996

1 3 5 7 9 10 8 6 4 2

© Paul Wilson 1996

Paul Wilson has asserted his right
under the Copyright, Designs and Patents Act 1988
to be identified as the author of this work

First published in the United Kingdom in 1996 by Jonathan Cape,
Random House, 20 Vauxhall Bridge Road, London SW 1V 2SA

Random House Australia (Pty) Limited
20 Alfred Street, Milsons Point, Sydney,
New South Wales 2061, Australia

Random House New Zealand Limited
18 Poland Road, Glenfield,
Auckland 10, New Zealand

Random House South Africa (Pty) Limited
PO Box 337, Bergvlei, 2012 South Africa

Random House UK Limited Reg. No. 954009

A CIP catalogue record for this book
is available from the British Library

Papers used by Random House UK Limited are natural,
recyclable products made from wood grown in sustainable forests.
The manufacturing processes conform to the environmental
regulations of the country of origin.

ISBN 0–224–04208–4

Printed and bound in Great Britain by
Mackays of Chatham PLC

For my sons, and the lives they'll live

I bequeath myself to the dirt to grow from the grass I love,
If you want me again look for me under your book-soles.
You will hardly know who I am or what I mean,
But I shall be good health to you nevertheless
and filter and fibre your blood.

Leaves of Grass by Walt Whitman

1   At the First Strike of the Earth

At the first strike of the earth a sigh is drawn from him. Ewan
McCarthy would say it is the physical act which draws it, not
some release of feeling, but who is to decide? The rains slant
gently into him. Ewan fancies it as derision. He settles the
spade on the ground again, then pushes with the sole of his
boot and cuts the earth. There – that sigh again.

2   When Ewan McCarthy Was Ten, the American Army Invaded

Ewan McCarthy never had a precise vision of where he was
heading in the world, except that he often had a dream which
finished with him in the morning, bolt upright, awake and
sweaty still, though what he remembered of the dream – the
swelling lights of a tidy house in the distance on a night when
the wind was scattering leaves – seemed to offer a kind of
promise. The morning after the first dream was the morning
the Americans arrived.

Ewan was ten when the American army invaded. It began
early that morning, on the edge of St Agnes, as a column of

soldiers marched past outside. Ewan could barely hear the marching. These men did not wear hobnail boots like the British soldiers did. The Americans moving in rank through the town didn't ring like steel on stone. Their real leather shoes made for a richer, softer smack over which Ewan McCarthy could hear distinctly the other more familiar sounds of morning and, rising above them all, the metronome call of the corporal: 'Lit ret, lit ret.'

Ewan watched them pass by below. That was glory, he thought, idling for the right word. That was style, he thought, as he stood at the window waving to the passing Americans for whom people had been waiting for as long as he could remember. His small white penis hung absently from the open fly of his pyjamas as he pressed his face against the glass.

For all his life after those months in 1944, whenever Ewan McCarthy heard words like steadfast, honourable, elegant, gracious, brave, he would bring to mind the Americans stationed in the fields above Mahoney's Wood. He would catch in his mind's eye that scene on the first morning: the low stamp of feet and the sweet-as-a-nut cry of the corporal which seemed to sing of hope and surety and brotherhood. The soldiers themselves, two days in England, were cold, scared, bored, horny and lost, but, for Ewan McCarthy, the world was as yet undamaged by such compromise.

Ewan McCarthy was an intense child who won a scholarship to the St Agnes Grammar School and grew into an apparently careful and amusing man steering a self-contained course through harbour waters. As he grew into his middle years, he took on the appearance more and more of a welcome character actor; he had a pleasant face and a role he was so familiar with that he never lost his lines or gave the audience cause for concern that he would be caught out, or that the plot line might become unthreaded through carelessness on his part. Ewan learned to judge the impact of all his sentences, such was his wish not to offend (unless it seemed a professional necessity). Along the way he picked up a private and solitary liking for jazz and met his wife and won a respectable degree, without astonishing anyone. Other than going away to qualify in law, he lived all his life in St Agnes and he became – has become – the kind of man who, if you had learned that he had done some remarkable thing like befriend unto death an American GI called Werbernuik (who had once built trawlers in Maine boatyards and sailed with whaling ships off New-foundland and sang the 'Marseillaise' full-throated one clean night on Hanover Hill while all the town below was hushed), or that he would stumble later upon some remarkable truth about his own life, you would remark, 'Who? Ewan McCarthy, the lawyer? Really?'

And yet, and yet – the lives which people inhabit, wear, breathe, are so different from the ones they are perceived as living that for Ewan McCarthy himself it had come as no surprise at all that in his sixtieth year he had recently been visited by the still thirty-four-year-old Private Sol Werber-nuik who had commanded him, as if Ewan were some latter-day Noah, to build a whaling ship on the farmland above St Agnes, Lancashire, to make her sailable and ready for the

3

sea and to name her *Good Hope* on the rising bow of the vessel.

3 Mapping Out the World

Sometimes he believed he could map out the geography of the whole world by the cases he had taken, so completely did his professional life seem to frame the extent of other men's absurdities. There was the old grain road where Solomon Heaney tried to kill his wife and failed; the reservoir, where Mrs Augee fell and left only chaos and questions behind; the park, where Denny Arkin shot eleven council ducks and sold them on and someone got lead poisoning and two others choked on the pellets left in the birds; the tenements, where Salazar lived and did things. And so on. Political men had victories and defeats for their charts. Women mapped out the world using navigational terms like marriage and love and birth. His map would be a map of the quiet desperation of his fellow citizens, but Ewan McCarthy had travelled hopefully.

Of course, the compromise came later, the offering up of parts of himself, some that he cherished. The feeling that he'd missed a turn or had become less than he might have been. Sometimes he worried that too much had been given away, and once or twice a year he'd worry about what was left and, with Ann gone to bed, he'd take refuge in the study and read Hemingway and drink Scotch or coffee and listen to John Coltrane playing 'Inch Worm' and Cole Porter tunes with his big dog sat close by him and imagine the swelling lights of a big house in the distance, and it would always seem a windy night for brave travellers outside.

Now and then St Agnes, which had had a smelting works in the town since 1810 and had the biggest single site production plant you ever saw, the Seebohm power station which ran on for four hundred acres, was voted amongst the top ten best towns to live in England. A group of academics in Cambridge published their list each year. They used all kinds of indicators and what helped St Agnes most was the low level of house prices, rainfall average, the way that professional men could live five miles out in the country and get to work with no great difficulty, the Civic Hall refurbished in 1900 by the Seebohms, the way motorways skirted the town but didn't interfere with life, the open-air market still running under the old clock tower, the Georgian terrace just off the High Street from where the town's four firms of lawyers practised and from where the annual Townsman's Guild procession could be seen to wind by on May Day. Some days a low mist hung over the town, making it seem to Ewan that the Bennet girls or a Mr Knightley would, likely as not, appear along Mahoney's track on a journey of marginal importance.

One place maybe not included in the Cambridge men's calculation was the five-acre zoo established in St Agnes in 1922 by one Jacob Seebohm after he had withdrawn from commerce. Unlike the Seebohm Plant, which the authorities were shortly due to sell back into private hands to a consortium who had experience of what was required, the zoo was set to shut for good this close season. So few people wanted to visit zoos these days, especially small, family-run zoos without gimmicks, without touch-and-feel or captive breeding claims or educational programmes. Now the zoo folk had run out of money and into debt and the dwindling band of animals was growing older and less anxious to oblige people by seeming alive.

Jacob Seebohm, founder of the zoo, was, before a parting of the ways, head of the family which had established and run the Seebohm Plant which was now being bought by a group of men whose administrative centre was in Berne, Switzerland, and who ran the Vorderrhein Project there in the mountains. Lately, and during negotiations, these new men came from Berne and all the bunting you could imagine was strung along the High Street, perhaps in gratitude for their investing in the ageing Plant and thus confirming that St Agnes would now and then still make some people's top ten.

Of course, St Agnes was not always so good a place to live for someone like Salazar. But then it was doubtful that the men in Cambridge had the Salazars and the Heaneys in mind; more the Ewan McCarthys of this world.

Ewan McCarthy knew his fellow citizens, working for the most part at the Seebohm Plant, pretty well. There weren't so many families in the town the firm hadn't represented or advised at some point over a will, a little conveyancing, a custody case, a defence, a prosecution. Ewan McCarthy saw familiar faces come in scared. Faces apprehensive of the law and of their chances. Ewan saw them through. Like Solomon Heaney's wife. She was in her forties the first time Ewan, by then a well-respected partner, represented her. Fat and in a big, flowered frock with wire wool hair, she said she loved food and ate till she was sick some days. She came to Ewan after her husband beat her up. She caught that sorrowful look in Ewan's eye.

'Once, I didn't look like this,' she said, and she and Ewan both knew that this was true. Her statement was a plea not to be judged, but she was too late. She had been judged in a way that Ewan himself could not be. By sheer dint of effort and the respect he had accrued, Ewan knew he was above the judgement poor souls like Mrs Heaney were open to.

Ewan never pictured himself as a good man. Just someone trying to live a reputable life according to the rules of others, and maybe in that he had succeeded, a man who didn't drink so much and was on three committees, and sometimes was sad about things long gone. He was perhaps at the solid centre of a good many people's worlds. That's how he saw himself (until recently, until the public meeting and what followed) – anchored, still and at the centre of things in St Agnes, with other men circling around him in their unsure and ambiguous and less perceptive orbits. The Townsman of the Year Award, with Ewan nominated by the St Agnes Chamber of Commerce, was surely the culmination of such steady progress through Ewan McCarthy's harbour waters.

It seemed on some days to Ewan that he had found a balance that had eluded others – Harris Leary, his erstwhile colleague, with the smell of embitterment about him; Mitch Murray, founder of the legal practice of which Ewan became a partner, who had made friends with the desolate around town but who was willing to sacrifice almost anything on the anvil of his sainthood including the uniqueness of his own children to him; his clients like Salazar, grown crooked in the half-light of their lives; the agitator Gabriel Snow, blighted by the need for revenge against the people at the Seebohm Plant who had dismissed him; his wife, whose need of Ewan could seem so unconsoling; his children, not always grateful and without the manners or the grace he'd been so keen to employ; and old Seebohm himself who had run away from the world and become saviour to a bunch of unnecessary animals.

Ewan had witnessed the scorn some people felt for Jacob Seebohm, for Mitch Murray, for others who so wanted love or respect, and he had come to base his life for want of something better on avoiding their mistakes. I am above that, Ewan thought. I am a survivor. I have made it through. I am triumphant. And so he was.

Even Ewan's fellow nominees this year for the Townsman of the Year Award and for the Felix Sommer trophy which the town gave with it (named after a former first citizen of the town) seemed coloured by their limitations – one girl in a wheelchair who'd mastered climbing a wall, two boys who'd rescued their father from a bathtub depth of water at the canal side, a piano teacher who preached at weekends, a business-man who'd been to Third World countries. Only Ewan's nomination seemed to indicate a sense of gratitude from the community which was wider than simple novelty or pity. Only Ewan's seemed to him to have about it, shall we say, that sense of the inevitable which came from the general, under-lying motion of a life. Only his seemed to be a recognition of

8

how at this point he had come to lie so near the centre of a stadium-full or more of St Agnes lives. Perhaps it would always be so, Ewan McCarthy can remember thinking.

4 Flying the Biplane

Some days he jogged, an older man in plimsolls and heavy woollen tracksuit, before running in St Agnes was fashionable. Slap, slap, slap – that's Ewan McCarthy, the solicitor. He took an hour at lunch between court and his afternoon string of clients, the Solomon Heaneys and Denny Arkins and Sala-zars of this world. He ran from the office, changed and hung his pressed suit in the top room which the firm, as it had prospered and spread across three facades on the terrace, had seen converted for the social use of the partners, through the recreation grounds and slowly up through Mahoney's Wood to the observation point, running above all dull men and the town, hitting absently through a hundred sifting thoughts; running with a swing of limbs that now and then in those last strides to the top shuddered into a flight of the spirit. A biplane of a thing he always thought. At his age. The way he ran. A shuddering wire-and-staple Sopwith Camel of a thing as he hit the final rise to the summit. Some days he laughed out loud.

5 The View across Town

Ewan McCarthy's was a roomy office with a view of the town and of Mahoney's Wood rising up beyond. It had been Mitch Murray's office but when Mitch died there was scope for one more partner in the firm and, with Harris Leary gone, Ewan was decisively next in line. The price to be paid was to take on Mitch's caseload. It wasn't of Ewan's choosing but it was possible in the end to get used to the Denny Arkins and the Solomon Heaneys even if you couldn't love them all as Mitch did. Mitch himself had four children and all of them, it seemed, had come to laugh at or be embarrassed by their father's need to have things done with such a sense of universal righteousness. All of them chose to deal with the world more man-to-man; to barter and exchange and so on. Ewan had come across the youngest son not too long ago running the timber yard in the town. An ark, of course, needs wood of various lengths.

'What would you want all that lot for?' the son had asked, amused and unconcerned as his sainted father would have been about unnerving clients. In response, Ewan had found no problem in lying, despite the sense he had of Mitch's hand on his shoulder as he spun some story he had worked on to explain the wood.

Ewan ran lunchtimes from his office. It wasn't every day these days, but it was enough to call it regular. It helped him to stay on top of things. It lent a balance to his days – he had a fear of toppling over into anything absurd or too unplanned.

It helped to deal with the frustrations of clients and cases. He took pleasure in the small disciplines of denial – of running when it was cold or wet, of going when he was tired or when he'd lost in court, of forcing himself the full three-and-a-half miles to the observation point and back to the office. It was never good for a man to have everything too easily; it left him a bystander in life. That's what he told the remaining partners those years ago before the partnership was offered to him on terms they knew he could afford and would accept, and his observation went down well as Ewan McCarthy surely knew it would.

When he'd hauled his way up to the observation point, panting like a terrier, he was left freewheeling, cleansed, back down into St Agnes town like he was taut and full of living still and not a foetus of a man curled into white sheets which is all there was of Mitch in the end the last time ordinary people saw him in the hospital.

6   Famous St Agnetians

St Agnes grew up on a confluence of six wooded hills (one less than Rome). A grain road, which was originally built by the Romans as they moved relentlessly north in that organised way of theirs, rose from the town and cut through them at their lowest northern point.

The people of St Agnes, Ewan McCarthy knew, were steadfast, happy to hold to routine, quick to mutter but slow to rebel. Their language was plain and soldierly. They might have a dozen words to denote rain or indebtedness but only one for love or fear. Words were pebbles, having a precise circumference, and what couldn't easily be reckoned was excluded. (Ewan McCarthy's words were subtler than his compatriots'. He had a softer, more worldly way of speaking. He could reach corners and find secrets that his foursquare, solid, fellow citizens could not get at. To be adept with words, no less than money, seemed a special blessing.)

In days gone by the people of St Agnes had been reluctant to support the Reformation but were against the subversion implied by the Pilgrimage of Grace; had been suspicious of Nonconformists, were Royalist against the extremes of a Cromwellian Parliament, and were famously unhappy to subscribe to Chartist fever abroad in the county – two brethren sent from Padiham were denied the opportunity of speaking at the Civic Hall on the subject and were driven out of town with sticks by the working men of St Agnes, who were happy enough, it seems, with Seebohm wages. Only once had passion overridden them – when Horace Weir, a travelling preacher, arrived in St Agnes in 1726 and set up his Salvationist Church in the stables of the Wheatsheaf Hotel behind the High Street and led the townsfolk into something like a maddened captivity for four months.

St Agnes is now known less for Horace Weir's strange and shortlived hold upon the town (begun when, early on, he wrestled with the town's typhus epidemic by turning it into a bear in full view of the gathered crowd and banishing it in the direction of Sabden), than for its freak low rainfall caused by the geography of the place, for its six geometric, wooded hills, for the manufacture of Seebohm energy which lights a dozen cities, for performing bears which were exhibited once at local fairs, for yielding one fine soprano who sang at Covent Garden and died full of youth and genius at forty-one; for a schoolboy St Agnetian who grew up to eat four of his lodgers one by one after administering soluble sodium cyanide.

St Agnes, through it all, got on with life and was sometimes voted in the Cambridge men's top ten. It was the kind of place where sometimes a banner was strung out across the High Street to advertise the Infirmary Gala or the Townsman of the Year Award in the belief that this would be sufficient. Not long ago, Ewan McCarthy's fellow citizens were, for one unsettling summer, the subject of a TV documentary series which, using fly-on-the-wall techniques, allowed ordinary men to talk about the issues which concerned them. St Agnes was perhaps identified as a representative and interesting kind of place, maybe by those same men in Cambridge. People were interviewed in pubs and clubs, in church halls and the like, allowed to ramble. Some people watched it through but Ewan McCarthy couldn't get on with it. It made the town, and him by implication, seem dull and introspective, wrapped up in irrelevancies against the wash of great events forming the backdrop to their views. It seemed unfair to do that to folk who truly were just doing their best, getting by – to let others tune in and turn preoccupation into sport.

They'd have been better showing the morning's procession of market stalls and noise like ribbon in the air. No one trying to be what they weren't. Just walking, standing. Just vaguely anxious and alive and wondering who'd shortly get the

Townsman of the Year Award, and bell claps from St Agnes' church and the sun warming the dry stone of the town.

7 Seebohm's Zoo

Winters from the age of twelve, the war over, the Americans gone, Ewan helped out at the zoo for Jacob Seebohm. During summer months there were always young men around to spend Easter to September labouring at the zoo, humping barrows of food and shit around. But when Jacob Seebohm's five acres just outside the town closed to the public after the season as it did each year and the boys went back to college or the city for the winter, Ewan reappeared, working weekends and holidays whilst his mother worked on in the café she ran, doing the odd jobs given him by Seebohm who'd taken a liking to him. Winters were best. In the aftermath of the Americans and of Sol Werbernuik, he was a boy in love with the distances that made him safe from people and from disappointment, but how to tell those who still wished to prime him with affection and flush him onto open ground?

He loved Seebohm's small zoo in winter – the rains on the empty perching slabs and the hardier animals puzzling in the outdoor silences and the three European wolves leaving paw prints in the snow fallen on their paddock. Besides, Ewan never went near the zoo in the daytime during the summer season. He liked it in the evenings when the last paying visitors had gone, when the wolves howled in celebration and the animals took up their natural lives. He liked it when the place could seem to be his, when it was all shut up and he could pretend it was his kingdom on all sides and there were no cries and scolding voices to dull the sounds of the animals and the air. Even then, Ewan McCarthy had discovered a gift for engineering the world to his own design.

Jacob Seebohm, an old man by then but still concerned with the welfare of the animals and of the zoo he had founded in 1922, gave Ewan special responsibility for the single spectacled bear. It had been the last of the St Agnes dancing bears – the ring inserted in its nose to induce pain if it displayed anything but passivity had been removed, though the memory of it surely remained – and Seebohm had taken pity on it. The post-war council, feeling perhaps that no bear or race should be so abused again, had finally removed the by-law which had permitted the practice of bears (with their teeth and claws removed) dancing for public entertainment. The bear-men's familiar cry of 'Catch a pole, bear' was vanquished, whereupon the spectacled bear's owner left town in disgust, abandoning the animal by tethering it to a lamp post in front of the Civic Hall.

Seebohm housed the bear in the penguin pit. It was meant to be a temporary measure following an outbreak of mumps that had wiped out his seven-strong penguin troupe. After that, though, Seebohm could never seem to afford to construct a purpose-built compound for the animal. All the interest from his trust fund for the zoo was taken up merely housing and feeding what he'd got already. And he couldn't have put the bear in with the three European wolves who had the only other paddock which would have sufficed – they would have ripped it to pieces, turned it into a domesticated jigsaw of a bear. So there it stayed, summers and winters in the penguin pit for twenty-one years, not content to die until the legal partnership in the firm of Murray Associates of its former ally in this world, Ewan McCarthy, had been conferred.

It was a sad kind of animal, turned grey by the shock of losing its owner, who'd meant the world to it. Through all its exhibited days in the zoo the bear had a habit of lumbering four steps forward from the back of the pit, stopping, then walking backwards to retrace the same four steps, then four forward, then four backwards. All day it did this, fascinating and appalling Ewan who, by experience and being around the bear, learned this: that two claps or a human yell seemed to wake the bear from this torment and set it dancing, or if a stick was thrown the bear would fetch it, or if the bear was hungry at that point it would beg, still moved as it was to perform to people who were embarrassed by so craven a display – especially because spectacled bears – the way their faces are patterned – seem so much more human than other species. No one except the appalled and fascinated Ewan stayed long by the penguin pit to watch the spectacled bear's attempts at dancing. There were few things so sad, Jacob Seebohm had remarked, as a three-hundred-pound bear looking for an audience. Other than this, when things fell quiet again, the bear would resume its vigil of four steps forward, four steps back. Ewan would go to feed the other animals and return when the zoo's visitors had gone at the end of the day, to find that, of all the animals, only the human-looking bear was unchanged, still in that one part of the pit, still stepping forward and back, forward and back, waiting for two claps or a yell.

8 The Principles of a Good Life

Ewan McCarthy had been born in St Agnes. He went away an
angular and unformed youth, to train in law and to marry and
then came back a citizen with a well-respected badge of
office. He brought up three sons of whom two were diligent
and worked hard at school, and the youngest at least never
robbed a bank or stayed silent for more than a week and was
his father's favourite, though Ewan never said as much to him.

There was no better feeling, Ewan McCarthy knew, than
being a well-liked man dealing in services that were respected
by the steadfast, working people of the town. He didn't mean
for this to flatter him, only that he understood and was
grateful that he had a talent which people valued: for having
old men talk to him respectfully; for being greeted in the
street by clients who had cause to be happy, by Salazar, slow
bear of a man, who frightened others; having a house on
the edge of town with a garden running some way back, a
cluster of beech trees and a single maple close to the patio; a
wife, grown sons, a big mongrel dog answering to 'Hemingway', who didn't take to strangers and who Ewan took for
walks late at night in the neighbourhood and who was easy
with Ewan's silences; for conferring easily with all and sundry
on football or on jurisprudence. What made it all the more so
was that lawyers, small-town lawyers anyhow, could appear to
small-town men to be priests of the community. His more
responsible colleagues and he were confessors, privy to a
hundred local secrets and deals. They were unnaturally

organised, surrounded by inventories of vice. They performed what seemed to people to be the intricate chants and mysteries of the courtroom: knowing when to rise, when to speak, when to fence clever in waiting rooms and when to hammer the opposition with bludgeon blows, which in a small town is how medieval monks must have seemed to blacksmiths. They had the power to bless and to absolve, and it was everything the young Ewan McCarthy had hoped it would be to lift him clear of the crowd. People might well have seen him in the street and believed that there went a contented man, and though they would have been off the mark it would not, until lately, have been by so very much.

9 Salazar's Bear

Salazar lived in one of the tenement blocks of flats behind the park that once had ducks. He hadn't always. Once he'd lived with his father but his father seemed intent on now and then having sex with him and inviting others round.

Salazar had, over the years, been locked up in psychiatric institutions out of town because he'd committed crimes that were believed to have been the result of his schizophrenia, which was itself foisted on him either at conception by his father's genes or by his inability to make sense of the disjointed world he later found around him. As Mitch Murray would have said, you pays your money and you takes your choice.

As for Salazar, his hero in all the world was the pressed-suited Ewan McCarthy who offered him absolution and coffee in his roomy office and good-natured debate on whether Dexter or May were better strikers of the ball than Gower, or Dalglish a better reader of the game from the front line than Puskas.

Ewan had given Salazar a job maintaining the garden behind the McCarthy house which Ewan hadn't the time or enough patience for, and which served at times to keep the big man out of trouble. Ewan paid him some amount per hour and Salazar worked until he dropped and waited for brews from the kitchen till he was offered them. One time they worked together on a rockery at the steep bottom end where the garden fell away to the back lane. Ewan chafed his fingers and cussed and hurt through the day. Salazar, though, was subdued in his intensity. It was, Ewan believed, a power and a solemnity which came from madness. Once, Salazar had beaten up a man who didn't walk again until the following spring. People knew that Ewan had given him this chance. There goes Ewan McCarthy, people said, saving the madman's soul.

Salazar had a theory that he was being stalked by a bear. A sly and surreptitious bear, this one. Not like the old St Agnes dancing bears who'd had their teeth and claws removed before their owners could obtain a licence for them to perform at fairs and at the three-day market, not like the abandoned creature old Seebohm had rescued after it had been tethered to the Civic Hall. He could talk quite easily about the bear in the middle of a conversation about some team's cup run or the repairs he was waiting for or the man upstairs who sometimes felt he saw spiders big as soup plates in his room – Salazar, with the cracked teeth and the basin fringe and the you-don't-quite-know-what-you-see grin he wore all the time except when he could sense the bear in the vicinity and when his fists, like knuckled hams, squeezed tension through him.

When Salazar started doing odd jobs for Ewan round at the house, Ewan's youngest, Tom, took to sitting with him. Tom, sixteen or seventeen then, and with no clear notion of where he was going or how he might choose to deal with the world other than through his music, seemed to share an affinity with Salazar. Ewan didn't know what they talked about, or whether they talked much at all. He would watch them through the window. Sometimes it bothered him in a way it didn't bother Ann, this kinship. Though he never said as much, he worried that Salazar's madness might somehow rub off accidentally onto Tom, who seemed so vulnerable to the world. Ewan knew that Ann saw this in his face, which made him deny it all the more when she asked.

'Leave them,' she would say. 'There's no harm in it. They like to sit together. I thought you liked Salazar?'

'I do. I do,' he said.

But Ewan could never quite bring his heart to trust the big bear absolutely with his son. There was always a residue of doubt. Once, Ewan knew, Salazar had glassed a man who'd been acquitted of buggering him, and Ewan put it down to that. It was fine for a man of Ewan's stature to grant Salazar patronage and absolution, but Tom was different, and Ewan sometimes found himself shouting down into the garden to Tom that the TV programme he'd mentioned he might watch was due to start, or that if Tom wanted to practise he'd better come and play the piano now before his mother went to bed. And if the boy yielded, Ewan felt a surge of gratitude for it, as he did whenever the boy yielded to him, as though he were surprised and amazed that the boy's stubbornness could be broken, and because he was safe now.

As we speak, Ewan McCarthy has little absolution left to offer. Things have changed and there is no going back. Not since the woman arrived at his office whose first words he can still recall:

'Mr McCarthy, you were recommended to me – I think you must help me.'

Until then, Ewan McCarthy had been invulnerable, safe in harbour waters. Now, though, he has sailed from port and discovered things are not now as they'd seemed to him.

Out in the fields over the town Ewan McCarthy strikes steadily at the soft earth, knowing for the first time in weeks what must be done.

10   The Art of Listening

'Mr McCarthy, you were recommended to me – I think you must help me.'

Her name was Rachel Tallow. Like Ewan, she had lived in St Agnes all her life, and Ewan knew why she was there. He knew what tack he'd follow with her case. He knew the probable outcome and the sense of gratitude she would come to feel she owed him for his help. See – blacksmith's magic.

21

Ewan can remember (even as he digs) that what struck him most was the inflexion in her voice, the way that she arranged her first sentence to show that she knew he was her man. She did not seem to him remarkably pretty, or forceful. How could he know the hold she would come to have upon his life? She looked the way people looked to Ewan McCarthy around town – as if she'd had five minutes less to fix her hair than she'd have liked, as if the coldness of the wind had taken her by surprise, as if she was due a new coat but was hanging on till Christmas. She wore a charm, a silver coin on a chain which she played with, a prayer for luck, or tolerance, or hope. She was younger than him, Ewan felt, but by how much it was difficult to say. A few years, ten perhaps. And she was, like most people, thrown a little off balance by the law firm's offices, the business of whispered litigation going on about her. But she looked for all the world like she would not surrender to her doubts about stepping in off the streets to pursue what she felt she needed to, the pressed-suited Ewan McCarthy saw. A file had already been prepared. The single word TALLOW had been marked in capitals on the folder which lay on the desk. Inside, there were some telephone numbers, some handwritten notes. 'Please,' Ewan said, 'take your time.'

His gift was in making clients feel at the centre of any conversation with him, no matter that he was in control. He knew she would tell him things he already knew. He knew there were quicker ways to make progress with the facts of the matter, but that wasn't Ewan McCarthy's way. He knew that this way she'd feel better, feel in charge of her situation, feel confident in Ewan McCarthy's handling of things. He sat back and waited for her and slowly Rachel Tallow set out her case.

Rachel Tallow's son had died a little over six months ago after a longish illness during which the man had come to be increasingly reliant on the nursing of his mother. Prior to his illness he had worked alongside his fellow St Agnetians for twelve years at the Seebohm Plant.

Now that he was gone she felt she wanted recompense for them both, and Mr McCarthy's name, she said, had been suggested to her. Ewan nodded acknowledgement at this. It turned out she held the Seebohm Plant somehow responsible for her son's death.

Rachel might know, Ewan suggested, that his firm had represented others in a similar position over the years. He gestured to a second file. She said that, yes, she knew. With some of the others, Ewan explained, Murray Associates had negotiated with the Seebohm Plant for *ex gratia* payments and for a reassessment of pension rights in line with the medical needs of the individual clients. All bar poor Mrs Augee, that was, whose dog was the only survivor of the dreadful accident. Any such payments, though, signalled no acceptance of culpability on the part of the Plant; they were merely a gesture each time from a patrician former employer. As such, these payments offered no assistance to any subsequent legal action such as the one Rachel Tallow was proposing. Also some claimants, aiming to take advantage of the Plant's willingness to talk, had been proved frauds and the nonsense had left a bad taste.

'I met Gabriel Snow,' Rachel Tallow said. 'He seemed a nice man.'

But Ewan knew what Gabriel Snow had been up to for years after getting fired from the Plant. 'I've heard he's something of a wreck,' Ewan said. 'I heard he was treated at the infirmary some of my clients have been treated at. Salazar tells me Gabriel Snow's had shock.'

'That's true,' she said, 'and he's still a nice man.'

'If I were you,' Ewan suggested, 'for the sake of your case, for the sake of your son, I'd keep at a distance from Gabriel Snow.'

'You think what he says might contaminate me?' Rachel Tallow asked.

'I think what he stands for might affect the chances of your case,' Ewan said.

Ewan asked her about payment made already by the Plant. Rachel Tallow said there had been an invalidity allowance paid to David, then a single lump sum after he died from the company pension fund.

'They offered me more money as – how did they put it? – relocation expenses,' she said, 'if I felt I wanted to move away from St Agnes, but I refused. Some would say that all of this was enough, but I regard it as modest in the aftermath of death.'

More notes to be made in the Tallow file. Some sums based on the figures she gave to him. Some medical details.

After a little calculation, and then making the first play of the cards he perceived them to hold, Ewan confessed that he thought that they stood a good chance of raising the one-off superannuation payment a good deal higher.

Rachel Tallow took it calmly but said that no, he didn't

understand. She didn't simply want more money. She wanted the whole thing out in the open. She wanted to sue. She wanted Ewan McCarthy's firm to sue the Seebohm Plant for the illness which killed her son. She wanted to shout about it from the rooftops.

Ewan indicated that he understood. Sensing a quickening tide, he stood back from cross-examining. They talked a little more, this time about St Agnes and about children and this and that until they found a door through which to steer a route to end the conversation, and Ewan McCarthy promised one more time to pursue the necessary strands of her case and call her back. And after she'd gone he wondered again why women in particular should seek to pin blame for cruel throws of nature's dice on tangible enemies they could beat and weep against, and knew his task would be to bring her round a little.

11   Dreaming of Iowa

Before all that, before Salazar and Mitch Murray and marriage and the house, before love and desire and the need to send people away grateful from his pleasant office and owing debts of allegiance, there was Sol Werbernuik and his soft leather shoes.

The first sighting of the Americans in St Agnes out of marching formation and away from the camp they had established in the fields up from Mahoney's Wood was when Lampeter's listless and scornful sister, working behind the bar of the Tavern on the High Street, watched two of them walk in through the side door one evening about six thirty.

The place was still empty. Old Ma Wark, who ran the Tavern for Felix Sommer (a man who had three butcher's shops and who was big in the Civic Society and in the Chamber of Commerce with his brother from the bank), had only just taken the latches off. The two Americans stood in the doorway giving the place the once-over. It was, she would say, like aliens landing. There they stood with MP on their mushroom hats and guns in their holsters. Ma Wark told people later that she didn't know whether to serve them or surrender. She was certainly felt by Lampeter's sister to have overplayed her hand. Whatever the truth may have been, she forgot to take the money for the beers they would drink at the table nearest to the bar.

'Gud eev'nin', Mai'm.'

They smiled their Brooklyn and Virginia smiles at the two women who, invaded, smiled back, and within a week the Tavern with its thick, maroon carpets, its coal fires and brasses on the walls, had become the regular base in the town for off-duty Americans from the camp.

Ewan McCarthy, ten years old and curious about uniforms and guns and the effect the Americans seemed to have on St Agnes folk (scorn and dizzy admiration in equal measure), heard the stories. Mostly he heard them in Lampeter's house, from Lampeter's sister and her girlfriends who talked in the front room or gathered in the kitchen on stools whilst Ewan and Lampeter, waiting for the war's end and cricket's return and wide, rolling, summer days, plotted the progress of the war on charts in corners of the house.

Lampeter was recovering from polio. He was confined to the house and Ewan was his one remaining visitor in this war-long convalescence, the two of them lying on the floor surrounded by test match score sheets and cigarette cards and the 1937 *Wisden* Ewan had bought second-hand with money from his father and which he had loaned to Lampeter to help pass the days. It was in this way, catching the edge of women's conversations, that Ewan learned about the Americans; that amongst the soldiers who began to frequent the Tavern were two twins of German origin from Wisconsin and that another, Indian Joe, would bite off the bottle tops of the beer with his beautiful teeth which made Ma Wark cringe, and two men from Boston were racketeers and conmen, and another – christened Handsome Bill – had been a college quarterback before he was drafted and who, six days after the invasion, was engaged to Lampeter's sister who felt the need to explain that she had lately found what she could only call a lust for life.

In all of this kerfuffle over the new arrivals, Ewan's mother was a reluctant player. Sylvie McCarthy ran the small café on the Padiham road at the edge of town. She was pleasant, of course, when the Americans began to make use of the café. They came in twos and threes to moon out of the window and dream of Iowa girls and she was happy for them, for their untainted lives, and for their money to go in the till, but what it meant is that it didn't change her life or the pace at which she breathed; nothing was awakened in her or made fearful.

Sylvie McCarthy had a life already set in place. She had already chased some small notions and had found herself, after being led by her husband into this and that, at what St Agnetians knew as the Last Chance Café – last house in town, last chance for food till Padiham, and her epitaph would be this: that men were clowns and dreams were foolish.

Sometimes, when she had gone virtually blind, when she was old and all but finished, or so it seemed to the lawyer Ewan McCarthy, she was taken out by Ewan in the car for a drive round the hill towns. Miles out from anywhere he recognised, with Ewan scanning junctions for a signpost to St Agnes or the Padiham road, they would round a corner and half-way along some drafty corridor of a street she'd say, 'There's a club just round that corner'. And they'd turn and there it would be, a bingo hall or a take-away now, but recognisably once a theatre or a hall, and she'd ask if they could stop a minute and she'd remember things as if by some sense of absorption, as if things past could seep back into her simply by her being there – blind and forty years on. Ewan would listen patiently, though with one eye on the time, and she would remember for him, arriving at venues drenched from the walk up from the bus stop and taking off her sodden stockings to dry on the radiator before she went on to sing to another audience of stern, white faces for ten and six a night. She would remember how at the Rialto, when 'Ramona' played there, that they put her up on stage to sing 'Only a Rose'. Would remember how in one backstage corridor (in several different venues according to Ewan's reckoning – it surely wasn't fair to keep a score –

which at various times she recalled was in Rochdale, Barnoldswick and Appleby to name just three) she'd been offered a spot on McNaughten's Circuit by a bald and sweating man who dabbed his forehead with a bright yellow handkerchief which he constantly took out from and put back in the breast pocket of his corduroy jacket. McNaughten's was the biggest club circuit in the north. To be invited on it was to be a sure-fire success, and she believed that her heart would never slow down again.

By then, of course, Sylvie had met Emmett McCarthy who, like her, worked at the Seebohm Plant but who had big plans and was keen to involve her in them. He had become her agent, persuading her that she would need someone to handle her growing bookings diary. He went on to promote her in local halls as 'The Nightingale McNaughten Couldn't Cage' after the McNaughten Circuit had withdrawn their offer over the terms Emmett McCarthy had demanded for them both.

'Don't worry,' Emmett had said. 'They'll be back, and then you'll be so happy we held out for all we could get from those shysters.'

Eventually Emmett McCarthy left the Seebohm Plant for good to become an agent full-time. He became an agent for others, including the woman in Euxton he would eventually leave Sylvie to live with. Sylvie never knew how he went about promoting the Euxton woman, though she could always imagine him doing it with that same gusto and lack of judgement. She understood from people that it didn't really work out in the end for him.

What stuck with her, she said, was that he'd had such a belief when he first met her that he was made for better things than he was mired in – working at the Seebohm Plant, seeing his life and that of others drip away without shape or form. Emmett McCarthy seemed so impressed with what he saw in me, Sylvie would say, and she would shake her head as if she could see the man, there and then, on that godforsaken street in some lost town she'd found herself in in Ewan's car. He was so plausible, she'd say, as if to excuse the fact that she'd been taken on board in her stupid, stupid youth by his scheming until the time that he abandoned her for good for the Euxton woman he'd been running around with. ('I'm her agent,' he'd say. 'I need to see her tonight, for the contracts. See! See!') He was so plausible and organised about his infidelity in a way that he never was in real life, leaving Sylvie running the café alone with just the Arkin girl for help (and, who knows, if he'd have asked her, maybe the Arkin girl would have gone too).

It seemed to Ewan some days in that wartime reign of the Americans that his mother was the only person alive who didn't wake each morning with the urgent recollection for one reason or another that the Yanks were here. She also seemed to be the only one who didn't work to turn out Seebohm power for the war effort at the Plant. She had, of course, worked there once alongside Ewan's father, who had dreamed of founding a casino or of rivalling the Seebohm place in business, of finding some talent to nurture through to theatrical stardom or of setting up a Last Chance Café on the edge of town where he and some fine woman would fry eggs together and look out at the hills.

They had bought the café, after the McNaughten dream had faded, using the nest egg left to her by her father, another Seebohm man who'd died of some cruel, invisible illness that made a mockery of his earlier fortitude. She had expressed a wish often enough to save it all, to keep it safe until her dreams were large enough to breathe life full into it, and maybe Emmett McCarthy did nothing more than wear her down little by little by little, persuading her that his dream of eggs and hills was hers, until she seemed daily to limp with hesitation and finally relented and spent it all on the café at the edge of town.

And so there she was, a woman with a son and a business leaking not just cash but the interest of her husband from the moment that the money was spent and the commitment made. Eventually, as war approached, the debts of the business overwhelmed her and the bank foreclosed. She was forced to sell, although the new owner, Felix Sommer, kept her on to run the place – her and the Arkin girl – and paid her a flat wage each week to run the place and to calculate his profit.

'She was a good parent because . . .' Ewan ran the thought round his head a lot when he was grown, half wondering and mystified what his own children thought of him. Years later, half-way through some court adjournment with Salazar and in a sea of graceless, straining faces, he completed the sentence:

' . . . because her dreams were all grown crooked and there were none left to saddle me with.'

The Americans, it should be said, had once again arrived too late.

Lampeter's house stood across the road from the makeshift parade ground the Americans used, which was the asphalt square beside the former Ragged School. Every morning a platoon of soldiers would be marched down from camp and along the High Street to be put through their drilling paces on the asphalt by a bellowing peacock corporal. Women and children gathered in doorways to watch from across the street – Felix Sommer's wife, Lampeter's sister and her friends, the Arkin girl with her dark hair and deep eyes who would marry Solomon Heaney and one day be dragged onto the moors by him and be left for dead, he not reckoning on her need to live and her hope for things to come.

Ewan and Lampeter watched from Lampeter's bedroom which overlooked the parade ground. Lampeter's room smelled of camphor and had the feel of sweat and condensation about it some days. The two of them drummed their fingers to the chorus snap of shoes outside until Lampeter became fatigued. They learned the calls of the drill men and the faces of the soldiers who lacked co-ordination and went white under the corporal's onslaught, and Ewan learned which ones were the regulars in the Tavern, which was Handsome Bill with the Clark Gable ears, and which were the Hoffman twins from Wisconsin whose father seemed to own the larger part of Milwaukee. And they watched the women of the street, the Arkin girl and the others, carry white enamel jugs across the road, from which they poured coffee, and they saw how the women became girls again as they served the soldiers.

Ewan McCarthy was sat by the window of the café looking
out from the seat that was his watching place. The café was
the last building on the road. The last house in St Agnes.
Beyond the Last Chance Café the road rose and buckled and
rose again straight as a die, as the Romans had intended it to,
until it cut the high edge of the horizon.

Ewan watched the line of the road. Did he blink? You
could not tell. Was he distracted or disturbed by the lorry
which had just rolled by. By the rain that flurried in no great
hurry against the window? Perhaps, although you could not
know for sure. Now and then he turned back to look around
the room. One time he seemed to notice the single customer
away at the front. Ewan examined him, unselfconsciously as
boys can do. Boys can see things as if they themselves are not
part of the equation, as if their presence is not adding to the
scene. Grown men especially, having forgotten, see it as bad
manners or challenging and feel the need for a joke or a wise
remark to fill the gnawing space, but Ewan wasn't challenging
anyone since he was hardly even there. He was searching
down that long St Agnes Roman road, expecting who knows
what.

Slowly, slowly, he returned. There was no hurry. At the age
of ten, with life an eternity just standing pond-still, there was
no hurry. The root of real innocence is lack of fear, and lack
of fear is born of eternity's promise that there will always be
another chance if needed, the promise that another turn will

fall to you wherever any single road forks into two or three and a choice is needed.

'Are you a Yank?'

Ewan's world was back inside the café. He was talking to the one customer his mother had. His mother was out back in the kitchen. The American soldier was bent over a book, absorbed in the slow turning of pages and the sipping of coffee. He looked up, seeming to notice the boy for the first time, and made a gesture with his shoulders which said, perhaps, 'I guess I probably am.' He went back to his book and Ewan's instinct was that he had found someone who hadn't made a joke or a wise remark.

Some time later, the coffee mostly gone, the American soldier said, 'You looking for something, kid?'

The soldier was smoking a cigarette. He was short and slightly built, wrapped on a wicker frame of a body, and he wore wire-rimmed spectacles on a boy's round face even though he was clearly older than most of the other GIs. Ewan sought to copy the same roll of the shoulders to say, 'I guess I could be doing something of that sort.' He looked back out of the window.

'Maybe you'll find it.'

'My dad.'

'Excuse me?'

'I'm waiting for my dad. This is where I wait for my dad.'

'Your dad away?'

'He's at the war.'

'You expecting him back on leave, then?'

'Maybe,' Ewan said. 'Sometimes he comes back and gives us money.'

'Us?'

'My mum and me. Last time, I bought a *Wisden*.'

The soldier nodded as though he understood, then went back to the last of his coffee. Another military truck rolled by from the town, heading out to the camp above Mahoney's Wood. After a while Ewan's mother appeared again at the counter and turned on the wireless low and a big band played a slow and peppery song, and it seemed in hindsight not so big a step at all from here that within a month Ewan McCarthy and Sol Werbernuik would be blood brothers.

13   The Dying of Strangers is Easy

The morning the truck ran off the road, they had met by chance on the grain road. Ewan sometimes walked up to Mahoney's Wood which, with the Americans camped out there, seemed to be the centre of the world.

There was a kind of security around the camp but nothing a ten-year-old boy couldn't undermine by asking to be allowed to walk round the back to watch the baseball game that ran in the field at the back of the bunk tents.

When the truck hit the trees just after the bend on the grain road running down from the camp it was doing perhaps fifty or fifty-five down the hill and there had been singing and tomfoolery and crashing gears in the cab. It was a strangely neutral thud, then silence as the engine cut, then after a moment someone crying. Ewan and Sol Werbernuik ran across together. Ewan remembers that he heard birdsong in the silence as he ran and that wheels were still spinning on the truck which lay on its side and that the wind blew fitfully. Birdsong while men bled to death still takes him by surprise when he thinks of it – the reaction of a boy who'd previously felt the world was more organised than this.

Handsome Bill was dead outright, as was the driver who Sol Werbernuik thought at first might be the salesman from Detroit but who turned out to be a farmer's boy. One Hoffman brother also seemed dead. The other had blood flowing from a gash which ran below his ear and was clutching his ribs and one leg seemed trapped and broken. He was screaming with pain and panic because he was surrounded by dead men in a wrecked truck. Sol Werbernuik tried to drag him clear but Hoffman just screamed all the louder and said his ribs hurt like hell and his leg was all chewed up and to get him out, but he wouldn't come, the leg wouldn't work loose, and in the end Sol Werbernuik, flushed with fear and sweat by now, swore at him and looked at a loss and seemed to want to weep at his own helplessness and only the presence of the boy held him there.

'What do we do, what do we do?' he asked, and Hoffman screamed louder and banged on the roof of the truck and swore at Sol Werbernuik and called him an arsehole faggot, and in the end what Sol Werbernuik elected to do was to run back up to camp and leave the boy with Hoffman because you got the sense that he had to do something and couldn't bear to do nothing and couldn't have the boy go and run for help which would have left him alone with the vile Hoffman.

'Faggot, faggot,' Hoffman screamed after him, crying with

pain all the while, and after that it was quiet again save for Hoffman's sobbing whilst Sol Werbernuik laboured up the hill for help and Ewan, left by the truck, sat cradling Hoffman's head and noticing how peaceful was the face of Handsome Bill right next to him and how little difference death had made other than an absence of breath and how unconcerned he'd seemed to be to die; how simple and undemonstrative a thing death was, like the cutting of a string. Later Ewan cried, when the military ambulance had gone and the truck had been winched free and towed back to camp and the world had moved on and when only he and Sol Werbernuik were left.

14 Arrivals in a Great City

How do you become grown-up?

They lay on the sluggish, half-growing, spring grass whilst Sol Werbernuik considered his question.

They were a few feet apart and at an angle to each other. Lampeter was weak again and confined to bed. It happened every now and then, pockets of sickness on his long slow push for recovery. As for Sol Werbernuik, off-duty he showed a preference to be either alone, usually in the café drinking coffee and reading a battered paperback, or with Ewan. His compatriots, he said, were moping for home or profit-mongering or cynical about the world, and he said it weighed down his spirit to be with them.

'I'll call you Nick Adams,' Sol Werbernuik said.

'Why?' said Ewan.

'It suits you. It's fitting. That's a good enough reason for something, isn't it?'

Though Ewan didn't understand why (any more than Sol Werbernuik truly understood the rules of cricket or the reason women in town called him 'love'), he accepted it as important to the American and answered to the name after that whenever Sol Werbernuik used it.

People were growing used to the American presence. To lorries and to men on exercises on the moors and to the marching by the Ragged School and to hothouse friendships growing fiercely as rumours of when the Allied invasion would be mounted came and ebbed and came again.

It was warm, Easter week. It had been the driest March for a hundred years. There was still a coolness, though, pressing at their shirts if they lay too long in one position or another and so every now and then they turned and stretched. Ewan McCarthy would remember that damp touching his side; he would sometimes reach for it in an absent moment in court; and in the years that would pass Ewan would remember Sol Werbernuik's answer in the way that some things said remain with you thirty years later having slotted into some place prepared for them, without effort or insistence – would remember it thus, not in words but in the textures that came before his senses filtered things into conformity . . . how do you become grown-up? It's that leap of imagination, as if you were arriving in a great city for the first time, maybe one suitcase in your hand and some dreams folded like money in your overcoat pocket . . . You feel the boom boom boom of your heart under a thick, winter shirt still sharp at the collar . . .

Your shoes were shiny when you left to start the journey here but now a thin film of dust suggests that you've met the first challenge somehow set for you.

You walk out of the station with the conviction that in years to come you'll be oblivious to these early heart-stopping city streets when you pass by – the height of some buildings, the noises of horns and newspaper-sellers – and you're happy because already you believe you're catching up on secrets.

You have an address. It means nothing to you as yet but you're determined not to seem too much the stranger to this indolent way of things and so you look and move from street to street urging yourself to stay casual and purposeful in the eyes of the city.

You pass face after face, the construction and set of which rings no bell of love or recognition but you continue in an act of faith which says that you will find the secret heart of some small handful of these people; will know some of them to smile at, buy regular groceries from, put bookshelves up for, share a taxi with, an evening, children, love and buttered toast with snow falling outside in the street.

Gradually you will come to know, and to forget you ever didn't, what the history is of that white building; what hold on the city's imagination that placid water has; how that man beat you to a promotion you deserved and how that woman over there let you down; will find what lies beyond those doors guarded by polished name plaques that for now are pushed shut to the public streets you walk along, bag in hand; will know that beyond this or that door is perhaps a red sofa or a hatstand on a patterned carpet. Until you find yourself one day somewhere near this same street and you are in some

mystical and appreciating way part of the picture – so that if
you chose to leave, to go back through that same station you
once arrived at when you carried that single suitcase and so
small a wad of dreams and not return, you'd leave a small hole
in the city's heart that no one else, not Roosevelt or William
Randolph Hearst or anyone, could fill with all the money or
investments they might have accrued in this same city, Sol
Werbernuik seemed to say, but that after that you must grow
old and start forgetting.

15   The Wrestling of Love to the Ground

In the café one day they became blood brothers, which is to
say that they each nicked the base of their thumbs with Sol
Werbernuik's Inuit knife and then clasped hands so that the
blood mingled in the grip that they held. The wireless on the
counter played bebop and the Arkin girl who was washing up
watched them through the serving hatch. Then, as blood
brothers, they shared secrets and Ewan's secret was this – that
his father wasn't at the war. This was a story used by Ewan and
his mother to explain the absence of his father, who was
presently living with a woman in Chorley who worked in the
Euxton munitions factory, and who (through the handling of
gunpowder there) had gone yellow. They talked about the
book Sol Werbernuik had been reading in the café for the last
few days. It was Hemingway and it was a man's book, they
agreed, because it was brave and honest and uncompromising

and therefore it meant nothing to women, or to those men who lived in packs for safety, and who had compromise written through them like letters through a stick of rock. At one point the group of four Americans who'd been sitting further down the café eating like pigs and making eyes at the Arkin girl got up to leave, and whooped and hollered slyly at Sol Werbernuik as they passed him and one cuffed him on the head.

After the four of them had gone, Sol Werbernuik saw the worry in the boy's face and smiled and said some men were like that when they came together. They were men who, when they went to a ball game, went like children to cheer the raucous winning of it and not to marvel at its grace or beauty, the earthy struggle, the pitch of emotion against daring. Singular men like he and Ewan couldn't let it worry them. They must make their own paths to follow, and they swore allegiance to all things brave, to Ernest Hemingway, to truth and to the sublimeness of great sport, and Sol Werbernuik promised that he'd learn a little cricket and that he'd show Ewan the rudiments of baseball and that before he left they'd play out the World Series on the open field by Mahoney's Wood above the town, but Ewan knew that blood brothers were forever and that Sol Werbernuik would never leave.

Love is so difficult to define. It's not as if you can wrestle or pin it to the floor (although some women believe you can – measure it, that is, and say, I love you more or less than I did then). But love, nevertheless, is close enough to what Ewan

McCarthy felt — some clumsy sense of being crucially alive and vital in another life. They lay there, finding ships and animals in the shape of the clouds that swung through the sky above them, and Sol Werbernuik spoke of how once the mizen-mast had snapped when they were two days out of Cape Breton and how two men died in the struggle to make for home.

16 Making His Way in the World

But when Ewan McCarthy came to make his way in the world it seemed that somehow he wasn't ready — not in the way he'd planned to be. Grammar-school boys became family-firm lawyers and town hall officials. It's just the way it went, pushed on by families anxious that no one should be left behind. Always, it seemed, there was some tide to catch and the fear of being left behind. Ewan would tell you it was his choice but then so would they all, the sturdy men in suits who in their forties became red-faced and defended themselves against change by remembering that they'd tried all this before.

Growing up truly took Ewan by surprise and he never recovered, so that for all his life he was compelled to hide his unreadiness by forgetting it and forgetting it harder and then some more. It wasn't that Sol Werbernuik had been disingenuous, more that Ewan had failed to make real the world he thought he'd seen ahead.

He did two years' National Service. He was stationed first at Catterick, then in Nuremberg. He sent his mother letters telling her in that frantic postcard way that he and the boys had eaten bratwurst and seen Russian soldiers and ridden the trams in Berlin and he was fine. He lost what little knowledge of the world he thought he'd once had. Or rather, he looked into the treasure chest one day and saw what he'd taken for treasure to be only rags – a compass that once perhaps had found Good Hope two days late, some Hemingway and an unstitched Whitman, a poor sketch of a bear in Jameson Land, an Eskimo knife, a short story, a smile on the end of a sentence that ran, 'I am a better man for finding you, Nick Adams,' the memory of soft leather shoes, some drilling and some death prevailed over, the map of a singular journey. It seemed poor currency in this different world of hard-nosed men, goodfellows who knew about everything that Ewan didn't – money, suits, how to plant five and make ten, how to fix a man. Here, Ewan's soft-bellied generosity could not prevail and, fearing he wouldn't make the journey, he turned for shore. He gave up, one by one, his notions of hitching across America, of writing a novel, of taking silk, of singing some damn fool song on any damn fool hill.

At Catterick the next bunk was taken by Libberman. Libberman spoke like a toff and finished up needing to answer to 'Toff' or 'Liverman' if he wished to answer at all and he became the hut scapegoat. Ewan spoke to him now and then, told Libberman he needed to join in with the swing of things if he was going to help himself, but Libberman never really

43

took him up and drifted further into himself. There was some incident in Nuremberg one night in the old part of the town where it was alleged that Libberman had been seen holding hands with a German youth and the boys in the barrack put him on trial and found him guilty and staged a fake hanging which they needn't have bothered about since before too long Libberman had done the job for them.

As for Ewan himself, he learned that he could hold men at bay by setting out for them how he'd cavorted with the Americans in '44, how Indian Joe had let him swig brandy and smoke cigars, how Stolley, the salesman from Detroit, had needed to cut him in after Ewan stumbled on their clever scams in the café, how the Hoffman twins from Wisconsin had crashed and limbs were ripped clean off, how Ewan had learned to smack home runs beyond the mess tents and the GI boys had called him 'Red' after some slugger back home. How he had followed their progress to Berlin as they were first brave and then drunk and enjoying the spoils of victory, drinking toasts, Ewan said, to the things they each had done and lambasting cowards and mess cooks and the like.

After that Ewan learned his trade, such as it was, well enough. He knew tort and contract. He studied the criminal law that he would hold ready for Salazar and Denny Arkin and the like, but all the time was nervous of the amateurishness of his own character – he believed throughout law school and while he served his articles with a city firm that if he were to audition for the part of Ewan McCarthy he'd fail. He began to run. Half a mile a day, in an old woollen tracksuit and plimsolls. There goes Ewan McCarthy, people said. A good, dull boy who stutters when he's nervous. Lacks experience as yet and hasn't learned to tell a tale. The trick, watching the goodfellows around him, had seemed to be to impress folk. He listed people in terms of those he needed to impress and those he didn't. He grew opinions on everything, mostly by reading the papers, and annoyed himself when these slid out of his recollection, leaving a hole where the opinion had been. He read books, good books, but his admiration for them dissipated by the second chapter and he gave up, each time sighing at the author's failure to keep the reader's attention gripped.

What finally helped was the safe attachment he formed with the first woman who was obviously attracted to him, a legal secretary in the firm called Ann who seemed to Ewan to have marked time waiting for him. Could that be possible? At least he deduced this from the way his life suddenly became easier in her presence. What finally helped was the respect his role in court and the suit won for him, although surely a partner-ship somewhere would give him a better footing still? It was then that a vacancy arose back in St Agnes (Ann who loved him was happy to go), and who wouldn't go back to the womb given so straight a choice?

Once back and under the limiting stewardship of Mitch Mur-ray, Ewan was free-er to invent himself anew. He became the local boy who'd been abroad to cities and the like, the lawyer and soon-to-be partner, and husband of Ann and junior states-man of St Agnes. Apart from Ann, of course, there was only he who knew that he'd never learned what lay beyond the doors he'd envied, never sailed boats and risked the snapping of the mizen-mast, never caught lobster, never sang the 'Marseillaise' on a clean night on Hanover Hill. For Ann, that lack was part of the whole of him and made him what he was.

Such things are not too difficult to set aside. One of the very few symptoms of this surrender was Ewan's lifelong need to maintain long lists of things to do and be — compass points, which he pinned up all around him: aims and objectives, ambitions, shopping, slights against him, enemies — as if the sun rising and setting were insufficient to guide him as he stepped through days that came like heartbeats, one after the other and indistinct.

Ewan took up with Harris Leary. They were a clever pair. Harris Leary was an able, young solicitor with a winning smile. He had a preference for suede shoes. He had the clean jawline of a sportsman. He played squash for the county on and off — Ewan played a little squash with him — and it was unfortunate that it took Harris Leary as long as it did in the end to realise that he wouldn't reach partner status in the firm.

Harris Leary didn't keep lists. Instead he worked on the disdain he seemed to show (but was unaware of) for anyone who wasn't him, which he maintained by making sure that in all conversations he never listened but simply rehearsed and sometimes started his next line. It was Ewan and Harris Leary together who coined the term 'swampman duty' for the free Saturday advice surgeries the firm began to hold on Mitch Murray's instructions. The firm (meaning Mitch himself) saw Harris Leary as lightweight and eventually had cause to deal with him over a well-documented incident with someone's wife. Mitch himself made Harris Leary resentful and moping whenever he was around. The other partners, of course, sided with Mitch however much they might smile at Harris Leary's dirty jokes and all the energy and foresight that Harris possessed begun to leak out corrosively as backroom sarcasm. All in all, he would have preferred to specialise in business contracts and to lunch with the St Agnes Chamber of Commerce but Harris Leary finally cooked his goose with that woman and Mitch Murray might have said that beggars couldn't be choosers.

17 Swampmen

The first time Ewan McCarthy met Salazar, some years after Mitch had died, he was on swampman duty and firmly established by now as a partner in the firm. Every Saturday morning the firm's solicitors still took turns to run the legal advice surgery in the office.

'THINK YOU'VE GOT A CASE?', the ad ran in the local paper every Friday night. It was an open surgery and free and quick. Fifteen-minute slots on more of a supermarket basis than old Mitch might have approved for those who couldn't afford to hire a lawyer by the hour.

Harris Leary, who loathed the surgeries from their early inception under Mitch Murray, had called it the baptising of the swampmen. He meant all those who were swamped by life, made lonesome and desperate by its circumstances, in need of any kind of advice and coffee and a listening ear from sympathetic men in pressed suits. The same faces kept showing up. The same lunacy. The same lives.

'I told you,' Harris Leary would say, 'swampmen!'

The spin-off was that the surgeries would sometimes snare clients who'd reappear later on with some other, more lucrative case or one which merited legal aid. Mostly, though, Saturdays were for people who'd been bitten by other people's dogs or by spiders big as soup plates, or wanting to file charges against the police or the bishop or to sue some television performer they'd never met for maintenance for their child. And it struck Ewan more than once that his living this satisfactory life was dependent upon his clients having no life at all. Harris Leary got one woman who maintained that her TV was emitting radiation and that if Harris just looked into her eyes he'd be able to see it, dancing as it were, on the surface of her retinas.

'What did you see?' Ewan asked gleefully.

'Whatever she wanted me to,' Harris Leary said, wearing that decorous smile of his.

18   The Business of the Day

It was always possible that distaste was written somewhere on Ewan McCarthy's face when he took up his chair on that first day Salazar appeared.

'Welcome to hell,' is how Salazar would always introduce

himself after that, breath smelling of pear drops, beaming like a child under that basin fringe as he filled the doorway.

Salazar was usually first in when it was Ewan McCarthy's turn to run the surgeries. Lord knows how long he'd queued – these were popular sessions. Behind him Ewan would hear the tired, mid-morning cry of babies and the shuffle of waiting feet from his clients with their unfinished, doughy faces, and although he always laughed off the remark and moved smoothly into the business of the day, Ewan knew that Salazar was right and this was hell and heaven was a squash court hour or a long drink with the dog sat close by him or the last sweating appointment leaving on a Friday night with a week in Corfu beckoning and the flight tonight from Manchester.

The business of the day was bears. Salazar wished to know on that first day if he could sue the people at Seebohm's Zoo for allowing their bear to escape and stalk him the way it did.

'What sort of bear?' Ewan asked politely.

Salazar grinned, his you-don't-quite-know-what-you-see grin. He didn't know. He said he never had got one clear look at it so far, it was too smart for that, though he was hopeful of catching a close-up view soon.

'What did the zoo say?' Ewan said.

'That they haven't got a bear. They're lying.'

Bears, Salazar said, were generally very smart. At least before their teeth and claws were pulled out and before the animals were taught to dance in the streets for crowds to watch, which seemed to have a dulling effect on their intelligence and ability to think clearly – to rationalise.

Perhaps Ewan was too kind, because Salazar certainly took a shine to him. Ewan said he would investigate, of course, and

Salazar said he didn't want a letter, that he'd be happy to come back and be first in the line next time Ewan McCarthy was on Saturday duty and hear the news from Ewan in person. Ewan took his name and details and said he'd get in touch with the people at the zoo whom he knew, and that if this was OK that Salazar's fifteen minutes were up.

Of course he didn't. Approaching the zoo was futile. He knew that the authorities there were telling the truth – that they'd had no bear since the old spectacled bear which had been in Ewan McCarthy's youthful charge had died shortly after Ewan had finally been made a partner in the legal firm of Murray Associates. Instead, Ewan entertained his colleagues with the case, then Ann (who wasn't as impressed as they), and finally he called the Housing Department and by a circuitous route found out that Salazar had a social worker. The social worker explained to Ewan that Salazar was deemed to have a coping mechanism whereby he would project out all the bad parts of himself onto an external object.

'The bear?' Ewan asked.

'That's right,' she said, 'the bear.'

She'd come over to his roomy office to talk and they drank coffee. She said it was a pleasant room. Nothing like the poky office she shared with the area social work team, nine of them and the pandemonium which ensued. The social worker liked the two prints on the wall. Ann had bought them in Italy one year for him, she said. She liked the view of the town Ewan had, and of Mahoney's Wood rising up beyond. Ewan mentioned he went running there. She crossed her nice legs and he couldn't help noticing but made efforts to show he hadn't.

'What bad things?' Ewan asked her.

'Bad feelings,' she said. 'Bad thoughts. Violent intentions. Perhaps originally they were directed at his father, but he daren't express them and has to find a home for them somewhere. An outlet. Now all the bad stuff in him goes the same way instead of being expressed appropriately, and Salazar can believe the same con trick he believed as a child – that he's a sweet guy in a happy-go-lucky world just being haunted now and then by a bear.'

Ewan McCarthy marvelled at how the fragmented world of a shambling and sometimes frightening man could be made so manageable by her. So understandable. He felt he really liked her. The way she looked at things offered so much wider a panorama of the world than Ann, who sometimes, Ewan felt, hadn't done much more than pin her life to his. Her name was Jenny Aldred. She earned for this kind of work only a third of what Ewan took home at that point as a senior partner in the firm of Murray Associates. She worked long hours and every day for her, from what he could glean, seemed pretty much a come-again-Saturday kind of day.

19   Standing for the Board of the St Agnes Night Shelter

'His own violence and adulthood frighten him,' Jenny Aldred once said as they were reviewing Salazar's case, as they frequently were after that.

'And whenever he does something bad, something violent, he believes it to be the bear?'

'That's right.' She was so grateful he'd understood. 'Or if something bad happens to him, it's the bear. Sometimes he will turn his anger on himself and claim it was this external thing, this bear.'

'What should I do?' Ewan asked. 'When he mentions it? The bear? Do I tell him I know it's not real? Reason with him?'

'I don't know,' she said. 'I don't think it would do much good. Not at this stage. You're the first person he's trusted, in donkey's years. However little you have done to merit it, you are his first good parent. To have his friendship, which seems important to him, you must accept him on his own terms. At the outset at least. After all, we each live in our own singular world, do we not?'

Ewan looked at her benignly.

'The bear,' she said, 'is as real as the St Agnes church tower in the world inhabited by Salazar.'

Ewan went along with Salazar, knowing all the time what was real and what was not, being the possessor of the secret key to the proper world shielded from the larger man. He persuaded Salazar thus: remember, he said, that there were people out there (magistrates, policemen, benefit clerks) who didn't know the bear story to be true as Ewan McCarthy did. For their benefit, there needed to be the pretence that there was no bear stalking Salazar. That, for such people, Salazar was a figure haunted by his own violence and unease and not by a surreptitious black bear escaping nightly from old Seebohm's ramshackle zoo on the edge of town. And so by feats of juggling and some hard work, largely on Jenny Aldred's part Ewan McCarthy was always in a hurry to assert, they kept Salazar out of prison for the most part. There was an occasional term in the St Agnes Night Shelter when Salazar was thrown out of lodgings, and just one admission to the psychiatric unit of the infirmary since the start of their alliance that first (for Ewan) come-again-Saturday. And on Saturdays, Salazar, beachball face and broken smile, would be first in line with some tale about the bear and Ewan would promise to investigate and then would say that Salazar's time was up and that Harris Leary's woman with the poisonous television was waiting to see him next.

It was some time after his first introduction to Salazar that Ewan McCarthy was persuaded by Jenny Aldred to stand for co-option onto the Board of Trustees of the St Agnes Night Shelter. Ewan was never too clear about his own motives in accepting the offer. Maybe it was just the simple tide to take. He knew it felt good to collect the plaudits of his fellows for being connected to a worthy cause. He knew they were grateful to have a legal man on the Board. And maybe there was just the vaguest sense of lust, if he was honest, if honesty was the right word, for Jenny Aldred, which he worked hard for a while to convert to an attraction to her personality, which espoused good causes. It did not harm in this respect that he had taken on Salazar at home as handyman and gardener and, in doing so, had tapped a strain of meekness in the big man in the face of the inexorable, seasonal clock which pushed out buds and leafed trees miraculously in front of him. (Eventually Salazar even got settled and more easy with Ewan's dog who never did like strangers and always woofed to its heart's content at Ewan's milkman and on Fridays when the bins were emptied.)

At the time the Tallow thing began Ewan was still on the Board, and the Night Shelter's work and reputation, and Ewan's for being a good fellow, were growing all around him. He continued to attend the quarterly meetings of the Board of Trustees, having discovered somewhat by accident early on in this period – after Jenny Aldred had turned down his advances – that it really was too late anyhow to retract his offer of help and go backing out of the venture without his action being interpreted as peevishness.

It was a momentary aberration in the clean lines of his life. It wasn't that he didn't love Ann. He did, he loved Ann. More that he fell into the thing with a colleague he respected and spent time around and maybe even misread the signs. She'd been so definite in turning him down that it felt like an accusation in itself, but she was surely wrong in this. It was possible, was it not, for two people working closely together to blunder into something in which no one was at fault (and Ann could still be said to be loved wholeheartedly) and then withdraw? Ewan managed in the end to put it down simply to misreading the signs. By the end of that month, gnawing on the situation like a well-chewed bone, it had become evident to him that Jenny Aldred was at least half to blame for signalling things he was at liberty to misconstrue. In fact from some angles he might seem the innocent party whose good character had been momentarily impugned – although he found it in him to forgive her role in all of this.

20 Lists

Ewan McCarthy, partner in the law firm of Murray Associates and married to Ann and with three sons now living more or less useful lives, was ever a man for lists. This one he wrote out not too long after Jenny Aldred had turned down his half-hearted approach and, half joking, pinned to the wall; it may be there still. Ewan was of the belief that any man drifting upwards needed a number of attributes and somewhere on the list (there he was again) was the kind of perspective that came from an orderly existence. He presumed that this need to have a perspective on things was Mitch Murray's influence – seeing as how Ewan McCarthy was Mitch Murray's protégé in the firm.

It was a strongly held belief in St Agnes that Mitch Murray was as near a saint as the town had seen, unlike the bogus Horace Weir. Half the town went to Mitch's funeral and, although Ewan McCarthy didn't entirely subscribe to the town's beatification of Mitch – who could sometimes in Ewan's opinion be a difficult man – Ewan confessed to people that it broke his heart that he couldn't be there too.

1 Be consistent
2 Always be ready to learn
3 Signal at junctions
4 Feed the dog
5 Do your share of the listening
6 Wear black shoes

7 Don't cheat on your wife or undermine your friends

8 Never wear a green tie with a blue suit

9 Avoid the lift if you can take the stairs

10 Give coins to winos, never notes

11 Check the ansaphone

12 Never do something with the sole intention of causing hurt

13 Remember the work it took to get here

He left it like that but, a few days later, worried about having it stand at thirteen, he added:

14 Be lucky

Except that Mitch Murray saw it one time and said something about luck being for the undeserving.

It should perhaps be said at this point that Ewan McCarthy could never have lived a truly good life. Not like Mitch Murray or Ewan's chaste and unhurried wife. Not since the unremarkable discovery made many years previously by Jacob Seebohm which was this – that Ewan McCarthy was a competent man, clever even, but lacking in a certain light a human heart. At the time Ewan felt, of course, that it must have taken a wicked man to say such a thing. And Seebohm after all was nothing more than some old man who had retreated from the world to run a zoo and who was angry, as though Ewan could be held responsible for what had happened. No heart – it was an absurd allegation. Seebohm was simply irked, Ewan felt, that the younger man didn't blub, thought things through, was well dug in, had some ambition to safeguard himself against flights of fancy, now and then held grudges against people who'd tried to bring harm to him.

Jacob Seebohm didn't seem to find Ewan's condition peculiar. Seebohm said that in his experience it was a common enough condition and that with a little work and some disguise Ewan would make it through without too many people finding him out. Ewan had, Seebohm felt, the manners to escape detection. Indeed, Seebohm said he'd only been moved to say what he had because of the promise the young man's life held, because of how so many lesser men fell short and how far in miles they finished from the beating centre of their real lives.

In fact, Ewan forgot all about Seebohm's diagnosis for many years until one day Mitch Murray, the nearest man to a saint St Agnes had seen, had cause to tell Ewan McCarthy quietly on his sickbed exactly what Jacob Seebohm had told Ewan all those years ago, and Ewan marvelled at how our lives are sometimes touched by coincidence.

21   The Bear Pit's Empty

Some weeks after Rachel Tallow had been to see him for the first time seeking to atone for the death of her son, Ewan McCarthy found himself being led round old Seebohm's five-acre zoo by Salazar. It was the day of the St Agnes Townsman of the Year Award for which Ewan had been nominated as one of a shortlist of six. The award was an annual promotion by the St Agnes Civic Society, sponsored by the Seebohm Plant, which bore the costs of the buffet and the Civic Hall dance. Though it meant nothing to anyone beyond the grain road, to St Agnetians the award was a familiar and reassuring point in the annual turn of the seasons.

It had taken little persuasion from Salazar for Ewan to agree to Salazar's request. Ewan was happy to be away from the office for an hour or two, away from the persistent wishes and good lucks of juniors and secretaries with their attendant risk of hubris, and from the leg-pulls of the other partners. And he wasn't unhappy to be back at the zoo. And the Tallow thing was progressing after he'd spoken to contacts at the Seebohm Plant (Rachel Tallow had rung twice and Ewan, sensing a little progress, had agreed to see her again). And he was feeling irked by Harris Leary the Fifth's office clowning. All juniors, seeming the same now, had become Harris Leary to him. Harris Leary Two, Three and Four had been and gone over the years. Harris Leary the Fifth was getting hard to live with. There was no court appearance today, and the air smelled good and the sky seemed high and wide and not at all oppressive and so Ewan went.

Ewan McCarthy, good Samaritan and wise counsel, pulled out his wallet at the zoo gates. There were few people about. Mrs Heaney in two cardigans in the entrance kiosk, half-way through a family pack of salt and vinegar crisps and with a theosophical tract folded open on the counter and scored in biro, seemed taken by surprise by their arrival but pleased enough in a non-commital way to see Ewan. She was well into her sixties now (that seven or eight years older than Ewan through her life), fat as ever of course, retired from the Seebohm Plant but still earning pin money mornings at the zoo and cleaning three evenings in a chemist shop and a doctor's surgery, defiant and just a little out of step with things. Ewan felt she must be grateful for having so quiet a time of it out here.

The news around town that this was undoubtedly the zoo's last season had done nothing to increase attendances, and so Ewan and Salazar could walk around the uncluttered concrete ramps and paths between railings and cages.

'This way,' Salazar said.

'I used to work here as a boy,' Ewan said. 'Did I ever tell you?'

'I didn't know, boss.'

Ewan had weaned Salazar onto 'boss'. Early on, Salazar had been intent on using 'sir' and saying it with such an obsequious tilt that it made the hairs stand up on Ewan McCarthy's neck.

'It was just after the war when I started,' Ewan said. 'When I was at school. I came up weekends and evenings to help out, through until I did my National Service and then went to college. I'll truly miss the place if it really does close up for good. I had good times here, mucking out and feeding the animals for old Jacob Seebohm.'

Ewan stroked the knuckles of his right hand as he spoke. They walked on towards the large animal paddocks which were Salazar's destination. They passed the only other two paying customers that morning: an old man by the reptile hut eating peanuts from a paper bag and, round another bend, a woman in a heavy coat and carrying a suitcase staring intently through the bars of a cage that seemed to have no animal in it, and Ewan felt that surge of elation which came from having precedence over a great and shambling wreck of a man who needed you, ship-anchor that you were, to hold his swaying life together.

'See,' said Salazar, 'the bear pit's empty.'

It wasn't the bear pit, of course, but the penguin pit, though it was indeed empty. The two men looked down from the viewing platform. It was the pit in which Jacob Seebohm had kept the spectacled bear for twenty-one years since he couldn't have put it in the paddock with the wolves who would have torn the toothless and abandoned creature to pieces even as it paced out its four steps forward and four back for ever more.

Over the last three or four years, as the proceeds from Seebohm's diminishing trust fund dwindled and finally dried up completely, the zoo's management had instituted a policy of accepting all reasonable offers for their exhibited animals in order to run down their stock levels. Now, as the closure date approached, the zoo was jettisoning animals to anyone who'd take them: baboons to Whipsnade, some reptiles to Blackpool, llamas to a farm in Scotland which was branching out that way.

'You're thinking that your bear was caged up here?' Ewan asked.

'Where else?' Salazar said.

'And you think it somehow managed to escape?' Ewan asked, playing along.

'Bears are very clever.'

Salazar explained how, before the zoo's pending closure became public, before people became aware that old Jacob Seebohm's trust fund for the animals was all used up, the bear would sneak out at night and torment Salazar and sneak back in before dawn. After each night that he had spent being stalked by the bear, after the bear had done things in his name or attacked him or wrecked the flat or scared the man upstairs, Salazar would come out here and the bear would, he sensed, be back in its pit, crouched inside the cave hollowed out at the back, large as life and nonchalant and ready for roll call as though it hadn't really helter-skeltered back in at dawn. (Ewan knew of course that there was no bear, that this pit had been empty for years.) Now however, Salazar reckoned, the bear had succeeded in getting out for good without being detected and with no alarm being raised, and it was able to haunt him any time of the day or night around St Agnes. Now the bear didn't have to race home to the zoo before dawn to ensure its nightly forays weren't discovered by the keepers. Now it was home free and Salazar's days were planned around the fear of being flushed out by the liberated bear onto open ground where, finally, there would be no cover to be had.

'Surely someone at the zoo would have noticed it had gone?' Ewan said, enjoying the sport a little.

Salazar said that no, with animals now being packed off all the time, being sent to other destinations, it could easily happen that one smart animal like the bear could make a run for it and have its absence put down to its being sold to another zoo or for dog food or something. After all, the sight of cages or pits or paddocks becoming suddenly empty was increasingly common. Admission prices had even been

61

cut in this last season precisely because of the diminishing stock of animals. The keepers could easily be led to believe that one more empty space meant simply one more sudden export, and who'd believe a madman like Salazar? You had to hand it to the bear, Salazar said. It had timed its run so well.

'I even saw it snooping round at your place when I was weeding the rockery,' Salazar said. 'That bear sniffs around wherever I damn well go.'

Ewan played along. It was a good theory, he felt forced to concede, well worked out, and it made it a straightforward exercise to console the haunted Salazar about it.

'I don't like it,' Salazar said. 'I don't like it that the bear has got clean away like this. This isn't any normal bear. It has become so much harder to be happy of late now that the bear is off curfew and free to stalk me any time.'

Ewan saw the sad and clumsy look on the man. How like Rachel Tallow's face it seemed, set in that same, determined, useful struggle to change circumstance and made lonesome and desperate by the fight.

'How to trap the bear?' Salazar said. 'How to get him off my back?'

They looked down into the empty pit. The hands of the giant Salazar, Ewan saw, were gripped tight like hams again.

'How's it look?'

'It looks fine.'

'You think it looks wrong, don't you?'

'Really, it's fine.'

'Well, I feel wrong in it.'

'There's nothing wrong with it. It's too late anyhow. We'll miss the citations.'

Ewan had been out in the garden inspecting Salazar's work, checking the summer jobs yet to be done. He liked the ritual it offered to him before supper. It helped to form the necessary barrier between work and the life that was his. He had worried once more about the maple and whether to leave it one more season or to bring it down and not risk the damage its roots might cause to the drainage.

And so they hurried across town, he and Ann, because the name Ewan McCarthy was included in the half-dozen nominations for Townsman of the Year, both knowing that Ann didn't look right, looking large and in a colour which hadn't helped after all. He didn't tell her. Marriage sometimes seemed to be the art of hatching small secrets in order to avoid the need for bigger ones. One such was this – that Ewan could be envious of other men whose wives, however fake, had style that clung about them whatever the season or what they wore. It wasn't a rampant or a physical envy. Not anything that ate at him inside or set him burning. What didn't help of course was that Ann, plain Ann, wouldn't always take him seriously, was so often somewhere in the wings smiling at the pantomime way of things instead of singing his song. God save me, Ewan McCarthy had been known to pray – what happened to unconditional love? He knew, begrudgingly, that she loved him. That was fine. Really, that was fine. It was just that sometimes, in that worn and refracted way in which things were unavoidably seen, it was tempting to want a little more, especially when you were Icarus, brave and flying high above the town, swooping now and then to rescue men from bears.

These things, though, remained secrets despite so many years of marriage and Saturdays and well-struck cases. Nothing so unusual in that. All of us are keepers of secrets behind the stillness of our public face – furtive and sometimes bent away from the light to hide our grief or insufficiency or loss. So when Ewan went that night, well-dressed and with his wife, to the Civic Hall, he was content that people saw what he wished them to see.

Which was what?

A man of steady influence, pleased in an amused kind of way that his name was on the shortlist people had come to honour. Happy in a fatherly fashion to see any of the names he was listed amongst collect the award.

But later, after the award had inexplicably gone to the girl who'd learned a little abseiling without the evident use of her legs and done some boating, Ewan couldn't help but feel a little curious that some teenager's tenuous claim could take precedence for people over the more substantial, steadier contribution to life in St Agnes of people like himself. This thought struck him most strongly after he'd been summoned to the police station at some time around three during the night, his dress suit (slung over the bedroom's wicker chair) still warm from the wearing, when Salazar had been caught apparently having broken into Jacob Seebohm's zoo and assaulted two officers in the process of arrest.

Ewan drove, red-eyed, tightness high in his stomach from the suddenness of waking to the phone call, his jacket pulled from the darkened wardrobe fastened to the throat against night. He was not militant or sour, but wondering how people could have got it wrong. The child who won was safely tucked in bed, not driving to the aid of a troubled fellow citizen. The child who'd won might contribute nothing more to St Agnes for the rest of her scrappy adolescence and beyond. He wasn't angry but he knew for sure that if the voters of the award could see him now at three in the morning, still not finished with the business of the day they would surely have taken more care over their decision. How's things?, people had asked at the Civic Hall all night as the evening wore on towards the announcement of the award. 'Are you and Ann keeping well? She looks well. She looks,' people said, 'alive and filled with purpose, do you know what we mean, Ewan? How's her work?'

They had asked about the boys as well. It was an extension of a good marriage that good boys would be a result, a kind of conclusion. Lawrence, the eldest, was now in Sussex and in publishing. Hugh taught at what his hypertensive wife always called a 'super school' in North Yorkshire. In adulthood both boys continued to be, as they always had been, neither difficult nor happy, nor obviously affectionate or indebted to Ewan when they came visiting, bringing their tribes of children, who wrecked the garden and sent Hemingway skulking down around the tool shed till dusk. In Hemingway's eyes, the only one worth a spit was Tom.

Sometimes Ewan told people that his marriage, any good marriage, was more than surface glitz and the cement of child rearing. This was the secret, he said, that there should be more to it than that. And each time through the evening when people asked after Ann (when she was talking to some other pair or at the buffet bar) she remained as well each time, he said, as content as anyone, as he, could wish in his description of her. Though if Ann were a colour, Ewan thought, she would be the colour of Aegean green he'd once seen in a winter sea, sometimes catching shafts of sun and appearing to be enviable but, on days when the sun was in offering, only a dull light and a darker texture. Sometimes it bothered Ewan that she didn't respect his work, his role, as much as he wanted her to, or when he performed some act of charity, for example, for the Night Shelter, when she simply smiled at his fuming over some magistrate's crassness or at some Harris Leary arsing around in the office. Sometimes it pained him that her life was his and that she seemed to take this on the chin. (A boxing metaphor, though, is surely misplaced for a couple who wrestled through marriage so very cordially.)

As he rose from his bed to attend to Salazar and justice, Ann had lain unmoving under the quilt, curled in a selfish warmth, though he guessed the phone and then his moving had woken her.

'Are you awake?'

She hadn't answered, lying impossibly still – a warmed stone – and in the morning she would say that she hadn't heard him get up. I know you are awake, he thought, though he said nothing else and dressed and locked the house up silently.

23   Chasing Phantoms

Ewan McCarthy, tendentious fighter for the poor, had risen from sleep. At three a.m. men in the police station dumbly went about their business with the hulabaloo subsided and shouts turned to sober sounds and creaks. Everyone knew the rest of the world to be in bed and ignorant of their business – every now and then a flurry of small activities, the bang of a door, a key, a raucous laugh, then that stubborn, night-time weightiness hanging on them again.

The two young coppers on the desk sympathised with Ewan. They called him 'sir', noticing that even dragged from the pit of his warm bed Ewan was uncreased, had found a clean shirt in the night after the phone line had gone dead again.

'Can't keep away,' they said, the two constables, fellow conspirators with their square and inexperienced faces – but you got the sense that they weren't so unhappy that someone else, someone well up in the rank of things, had been forced up into the night.

'It's your mate again,' they said, meaning Salazar. 'I'd get him off your list if I was you, sir. More trouble than he's worth, that one.' Policemen, Ewan thought, were happy to make clever remarks but expected you to do the smiling.

No, I like him. I feel I need to help. I am the last card he has left to play. That was the inference Ewan hoped to give. Ewan McCarthy, public servant, pressed on. A sergeant appeared.

'I expect you were at the Civic Hall tonight, sir?'

Ewan said he was.

'Good time?'

Ewan said he had. A good time. In moderation. We couldn't all go crazy. We couldn't all go chasing phantoms through the streets like Salazar, noisily and with no regard for the consequences or the well-being of the community. And in return? In return, it was true, there were compensations for the Ewan McCarthys of this world for being prepared to be wrenched sober from bed at three a.m.

The sergeant, mentioning the awards again, sympathised with Ewan. 'You'd have got my vote, sir. But then you'll not be missing sleep over it I guess.'

Ewan smiled and the sergeant led him, clattering, through a punchpad system, two locked doors and down a flight of hard stairs. Doors open for me, was the one dull thought that slid out into the night from Ewan McCarthy's separate and private world.

Salazar was sitting with his back hard up against the cell wall, the last survivor of an unnoticed shipwreck. Ewan could smell the drink on him.

'What have you boozed?'

'One and a half.'

'Shit.'

'There's some left in the second bottle,' Salazar said in mitigation.

Ewan sat on the end of the padded bench. 'So. Spill the beans. I thought we'd got away from all this.'

'I'm sorry, boss. I'm fucking sorry.'

Salazar belched and then, a moment after, farted. The sergeant made a move towards him but Ewan signalled, spread out the fingers of his slightly raised hand, and asked if the man could leave them for just a few minutes so that he, Ewan, could talk to his client alone. 'I'll be alright,' Ewan said.

'What were you doing at the zoo?' Ewan asked when they were alone.

'I thought you were supposed to defend me. I thought we could claim it wasn't me. Mistaken identity.'

'Look, it's half-way between bloody late and bloody early, and with a bit of luck I might get another hour in bed before I'm up again if I can get this sorted fast enough. Now what in Christ's name were you doing at the zoo at one in the morning? The police think you were thieving.'

'I found something out,' Salazar said. He was sobered a little by Ewan's urgency and, in fits and starts, he told his tale.

Salazar had got drunk, worried about the bear some more, then broken into the zoo earlier that night. Wandering around inside the zoo he had eventually discovered, he said, a pile of bones and savaged flesh in one of the unused courtyards which had at one time been a Pets Corner. It had four stables enclosing the small courtyard and was cordoned off to the public these days.

'I'm telling you,' he said, sounding slow and morose and wary of what he'd found out, 'I think the bear's done it. It's got back into the zoo grounds somehow and gone berserk. There were ripped-up skulls and rib cages with flesh torn off the bones. Oh God, boss, you never saw anything like it. You'd have drunk a bottle with me if you'd have seen. Piles of rotting animals that the bear's murdered in secret and no one's discovered. Oh Christ, and now it's got a real taste for blood. You tell the keepers, boss. They'll believe you. They've got to find a way to stop it or else the bear will start going for people. This is no normal bear. I kept saying this was no normal bear. No normal bear could have done this. You know what this bear is, boss. This is Horace Weir's bear come back. This is a bad omen for the town. Bad things coming. Horace Weir's fucking bear, just like he said – that's what it is. And when I tried to raise the alarm about what the bear had done they arrested me for breaking in. As if I didn't have more important things to do.'

Salazar sighed, and later he brought up the idea that if nothing was done about this bear (a bear first been seen in the town in 1727 after Horace Weir had conjured it from the town's typhus and banished it Sabden way), he would go to the press and get them to report on the animal so that people in the town could see what things were going on.

Beyond the window of Ewan McCarthy's office, Mahoney's Wood rose up a furlong away as steadily as it always had. Whilst generations of people worried about love and loss and bears, things stayed the same.

Rachel Tallow arrived a few moments late. She'd taken a little more care dressing, Ewan felt. That was good. A sense of balance in the way she managed things was a useful tool in a steady, unyielding world and it would serve them both well.

'I heard you almost won the Townsman of the Year Award last night,' she said.

'There were all kinds of fine candidates.'

'The girl from Sabden Heights won?'

'Yes,' he said. 'The one who took up outward bound after her accident.'

'Remarkable,' Rachel Tallow said as Ewan indicated for her to sit.

'Remarkable?'

'That anyone should possess such singular courage to do such things. And now to take up coaching others. Remarkable.'

'Yes,' Ewan said.

'To take such a grip on life and not just be swept along by circumstance.'

'She was a deserving winner,' Ewan said.

Rachel Tallow settled herself in the chair. 'St Agnes must

think a lot of you to see you nominated amongst people like that for your quieter services.'

'Perhaps it was just my turn,' Ewan suggested. 'Sometimes these things work like that. This year a lawyer, next year a businessman, then a councillor.'

'You're being disingenuous. I'm sure they chose you because they felt you were deserving of it.'

'I'm happy that they chose me, Mrs Tallow, and now I'm happy that it's all over and we can all get back to normal.' Ewan leant forward in his chair as if to conclude the whole puzzling and irrelevant sideshow and move on with life.

'And now I've chosen you,' she said.

Ewan had already spoken to Jenny Aldred about Salazar that morning, but he had been left disappointed. Perhaps he had been too merry on the phone, his head still light from lack of sleep. He had wanted to banter with her. He had wanted her to smile along with him about Salazar, the jester, bursting into the zoo and finding carcasses.

'I rang the zoo,' he had told Jenny Aldred. 'Do you know what they were? Animal remains cut up by the vet and the zoo staff. They cut them down to the bone, anything that dies on them, joint them nearly, looking for the cause of death and anything else that might be useful. Rooting in the entrails. That's what our boy stumbled on last night, so now he's running round believing his bear did it.'

There was no answer.

'Hallo, Jenny? Are you still with me?'

'I'm still here.' But the manner of her reply said that she wasn't with him on this one. She had been called to the phone from a meeting and Ewan wondered if perhaps it hadn't been going so well. He could just picture her in that oh-so-frantic office.

'And what did you say to him?' she said. He wondered if there were others present around her, people who she felt more closely allied to than him, and he began to feel an edge of resentment because it was she who was misjudging this conversation, not him.

'Well, nothing,' Ewan observed. 'I thought I should just play along with him. Since I wasn't his caseworker or anything. Just to go along with what he said.'

'That lets you nicely off the hook then, doesn't it?'

He thought she sounded a little tired, ragged. And when the conversation ended he realised that he was still unburdened of several sections of the passage of incidents he had wanted to relay to her. And on top of that, he was curious and unsatisfied that she hadn't mentioned the Townsman of the Year Award. She had been preoccupied with Salazar. Ewan felt that she was brandishing their client in front of him. She felt bad, she said, that she'd made so little progress, that she'd been unable to challenge the preconceptions which were starting to impinge again on Salazar's quality of life. Maybe, she said, thinking out loud, she should hospitalise him for a while again. Or risk some group therapy to confront his delusions head-on.

'Is that wise?' Ewan asked.

'I don't know,' she said. 'Truly, I don't know. Whatever the rights and wrongs, it's obvious he isn't ever going to come to terms unilaterally with the bear psychosis. You will find this a surprising admission, Ewan, but there are some of us out in the real world, poor wretches that we are, who sometimes feel compelled to make decisions based on nothing more than hope or desperation.'

25   Considering the Case against Us

'Mrs. Tallow, let me tell you how far we've come.'

Ewan opened the file and smiled as if to reassure her that all would be well, and who could have imagined at this stage that the hour would end prematurely with Ewan's client cursing and straining against his words and with her getting up to leave so abruptly and with the firm slapping of a door dead shut.

Ewan ran through the initial motions the firm had gone through in support of Rachel Tallow's case. He reviewed the correspondence with two reputable scientists the firm had consulted and with Harris Leary who represented the Seebohm Plant locally as part of their legal and public relations team.

'In addition I have some information from your son's specialist at the infirmary in the file somewhere which is also quite helpful.' On cue, Ewan found the paper, held it up, then replaced it on the table.

'So let me, if I may, précis things as they seem to stand at present – and you must correct me at any stage if you feel the need.'

He flipped again through sheets of paper until he found one that seemed in accord with what he wanted to say.

'Here we are. Now then. Right, so on the one hand, on our side you might say, is our assertion that your son was the victim of a degree of negligence on the part of the authorities at the Seebohm Plant, a negligence which we are wishing to allege was responsible for the onset of the leukaemia which was to be the eventual cause, some time after he ceased working at the Plant, of your son's death in ah, let me see . . . February of last year.'

He glanced up to Rachel Tallow who made no move to intervene. 'We are wanting to allege that the origins of the leukaemia lie in a long-term exposure to unacceptable levels of radiation at the Plant.'

'It started in 1987,' she said.

'I'm sorry?'

'It started in 1987. There was a drop in pressure in one of the reactors. Gasses were released. David was on duty that night. He saw the readings.'

'I've spoken to the Plant. They know about that story. It was just malicious. The readings show nothing unusual at that time.'

'There are figures missing.'

'Those are irrelevant,' Ewan said. 'They are for a different part of the Plant. I've seen them. Loesser's shown them to me. I've been through them with a technical consultant.'

'Nominated by the Plant.'

'Yes, nominated by the Plant but he is independent. He has interpreted the readings, the figures for us . . . '

'There was a release,' Rachel Tallow said, interrupting. 'Nine months later, David's leukaemia was first diagnosed.'

'. . . and what the consultant suggests is that there is insufficient data about a possible single release on which to build a case.'

'What are you saying?'

'I am saying, I am proposing, that if we do elect to argue your case with the Plant then we argue on the basis of protracted, low grade emissions over a number of years which could have precipitated the illness.'

'That wouldn't be as harmful to the Plant, would it? It would be less of an obstacle to the sale of the Plant.'

'It would offer you the best chance of getting something – to argue for an exposure potentially sufficient to induce the cancer which led to his retirement on health grounds. In support of our case, we would have at our disposal the medical evidence of the doctors who treated your son and who, amongst other things, would testify that the onset of the illness was indeed during your son's time at the Plant. For our purposes at least, that would lay the foundations of a circumstantial case. Further to that, we could bring evidence to court of levels of radiation within the Plant which at least some medical opinion would, we know, be prepared to testify is sufficiently high in certain circumstances to create an unacceptable risk in terms of its potential for inducing cancers.'

'I see,' Rachel Tallow said. Then she said, 'If he had been an accountant or a solicitor he would still be alive.'

Ewan wondered if that were an accident of words.

'But he is not alive,' she said. 'He is dead, and I am alone in the world. Do you know what that feels like, Mr McCarthy?'

Ewan, patient, cautious of upsetting the apple-cart, bowed his head, then lifted it to agree that she had experienced a dreadful year, one that any person would find it difficult to come through, and he left a pause here and there until he felt that his client was steadied and compliant again.

'Now,' he said, 'if we are going to mount a case which is to be effective we must carefully consider, as it were, the other side – the case which is against us and which we must be in a position to counter. You understand my meaning?'

'Yes, I understand.'

'Very well. As it now stands, the thrust of any case of ours would be countered by three arguments put forward on the part of the authorities at the Plant. I will endeavour to set out each of these three arguments which the Plant would be likely to mount and then perhaps, with everything on the table, we can sensibly review where we stand and what our next move might be.'

Rachel Tallow nodded.

'Firstly we have the problem of what is called linkage.'

'I know about linkage,' she said. 'I've read about similar cases since David died.'

'Good. Good. You will have a perception, then, of the measure of our task in seeking to prove satisfactorily to the court that your son's, ah, condition, was caused by the Plant. The authorities will, of course, sympathise over the illness which led to his death, will even offer a one-off payment as a gesture of good faith to an ex-employee stricken down by an act of God, but they will undoubtedly argue that there was no proven link between his illness and his previous work at the Plant – that he was unfortunate in developing the illness but that like others up and down the country it was one which had nothing to do with the Seebohm Plant. You understand?'

She is sitting so still, Ewan was thinking. I wish she would move just a little, just fidget or ask to smoke or for a glass of water. But she asked for nothing, just sought to take in and to sieve the meaning from each sentence.

'The second defence which they will raise concerns the levels of radiation at the Plant. They will not dispute that radiation exists as part of the process there. But they will say that all official readings taken within or near the Plant fall entirely within the limits set by the regulatory authorities governing the industry and which are recognised as safe. How can we be negligent, they will argue, when all we have done is to conform with the independently set safety levels for the industry?'

'They will say that the bulk of credible scientific evidence confirms the safety under operational conditions of this kind of facility. Only the discredited, the dispossessed and the crackpot are likely to oppose this data, they will assert. Or those with vendettas against their reasonable and necessary work. And look at our own record, they will say: no fatalities with a proven link to the Plant, no suggestion of environmental radiation, no guilt proven in any court of law. We are safe and responsible and an asset to the community, they will say.'

'I do not believe . . .' Rachel Tallow began, and Ewan was forced to intervene to quieten her.

'Please, just let me finish setting out all the cards on the table as we agreed,' and his hand stayed up a moment longer until she nodded and sat back.

'And thirdly,' Ewan said, 'in seeking to undermine the credibility which your case undoubtedly deserves, they may well choose to bring up the matter of Helen.'

'My sister?'

Ewan sifted for another document. 'Your sister died some years ago?'

'Yes. Yes she did.'

'And she died of leukaemia?'

'Yes.'

'And although she lived in St Agnes she was not herself at any stage exposed to the working routines inside the Plant which you want to argue caused your son's illness.'

'No, of course not. Helen never worked at the Plant.'

'You see, I have no doubt that the authorities at the Plant would choose to use such information to argue that your son was already susceptible at some genetic level to the illness before he ever set foot in the Seebohm Plant.'

'My sister's death has nothing to do with this.'

'I'm sure that is true,' Ewan said. 'Although it remains the case that our opponents would argue strongly in court that it did. And I'm sure you see that, if nothing else, this assemblage of issues does present us at the very least with a tactical difficulty to be overcome were we ever to elect to go to court to take on the Plant rather than seek to deal face to face with them in private.'

'David's death was caused by the Plant,' Rachel Tallow said. She had such bleak certainty, Ewan saw. She was so wilful, so . . . precise.

'I will take them on,' she said, 'and I will prove what I must prove. That's why I've chosen you.'

It was quiet after she had gone. Ewan looked out of the window, up to Mahoney's Wood, for a long time afterwards. He was unsure about what he felt; some sense of chaos, of disorder, which lay down in his stomach and weighed heavily. He had not fought her, that was not his way, but her intensity (when he had persisted that they petition for a quieter settlement out of court and he had mentioned figures he had already sounded out with Harris Leary and the rest of Loesser's team at the Plant) and finally her scorn had bruised him. And what he felt inside was the swelling of that bruise. He had, as gently as he could, tried to open up the threadbare and legally insubstantial nature of her case and his only mistake, if he had made one, had been to urge her too fulsomely to let her son be, and to go on with life anew; to take what she could from the Seebohm Plant and maybe even think of moving on from St Agnes if that would help to piece her life together again.

That lunchtime he ran, slowly and deliberately up the track, around the observation point and down, and the wind blew and soothed him. His life had been spent in the patient alchemy of turning base, shapeless instincts of anger and pride and revenge into sleek and glinting arguments for the court. But with Rachel Tallow there had been no alchemy. There was still only anger and a woman's dull need for revenge. Later, he had rung Loesser's office at the Plant and had spoken to Harris Leary.

'You're quiet', Ann said.

'Yes,' he said, uncomforted.

'You've been like that all evening. Why don't you listen to some music? Go and have a run.'

'I don't want a run.'

Ewan was surprised it was still with him, this sense of unease and unfulfilment. More usually he could put aside a day's confusion. He was intolerant of the weariness, the gravity that always seemed to follow the Jenny Aldreds of this world, mired in their indulgent need to go about rescuing swamp-men night and day.

'I want to help,' Ann said.

'I have to go and see Loesser and Harris Leary tomorrow about the Tallow thing. You know what they're like. They'll be busy alluding ruefully to the Vorderrhein people and the need for a smooth run-up to the sale of the Plant.'

'What will you tell them?' Ann asked.

'I don't know,' he said. 'That I couldn't persuade her to go for a deal. That she probably won't come back to me after what she said today. That she's a loose cannon now.' Ewan felt for the dog who was sat down by the chair, and rubbed the animal's snout. The dog sighed.

'She wouldn't take your advice?'

'I had to tell her that it was unlikely she'd get legal aid if she took it to court. She ended up behaving as though I were the enemy.'

'She wouldn't toe the reasonable line?'

'You sound like you're not on my side.'

'No, no, I didn't say that.'

'I've done what I can for her. Whatever case she has, and

81

it's not enough, wouldn't get her anywhere, and it might end up costing her everything – her capital, her house, everything. I've seen people like that before. I've seen them gamble and lose everything. Dash themselves on the rocks.'

'Perhaps she has nothing left to lose.'

'I don't know what that means,' Ewan said.

He stood up. 'I'm going to get Salazar to cut that maple down next week. I keep thinking we should have it done before it starts damaging the drains at this end of the house.'

'You know what,' Ann said, declining to end the conversation just yet.

'What?'

'About the Tallow case.'

'What about it?'

'You didn't mention her son. In an hour of talking about the case, you haven't once mentioned her son. I don't even know his name.'

'His name is David.'

'Was.'

'His name was David. So? Her son isn't my client. She is.'

'It's just that you complain that you don't understand her. And it's just – don't believe she'll ever make much sense to you unless you can feel some of her pain. Or at least see it.'

'Don't lecture me, Ann. I'm not a child.'

'No,' she said, 'you're not a child.'

In so many years that it bewildered him, he and Ann had only once fought badly enough for it to threaten their marriage. Ewan was no lover of scenes. In the aftermath of that one particular fight Ann had packed a small case and stayed overnight in a hotel out of town. The boys, Hugh and Lawrence at least, put down anchor in their rooms and skirmished with each other. Only Tom stayed around downstairs, as if he were measuring things up. After tea he played some piano practice, Ewan remembered. Some Thelonius Monk thing he was trying to pick up to the distaste of his piano teacher. He didn't say much, neither then nor when Ann returned, just watched them both with those big, hawk eyes. The following morning Ann had rung and Ewan had gone to collect her, and like well-adjusted adults they had found the space, or maybe the need, in which to become reconciled, and they had got on with their lives. That was how Ewan remembered it. During the row she said that sometimes, often, he didn't see what could be seen, feel what others felt. Not maliciously. Just . . . didn't see. The world, she said, could sometimes be said to be a set of two-dimensional, bit players in Ewan McCarthy's universe. Don't be perverse, he said, that's how the whole world went about its daily business. People preferring on instinct the destruction of the world to the scratching of their hand or an incidental accusation against them substantiated. It was just that some people were too proud to say it, or too conceited.

'If I bled for everyone, where would that get us?' Ewan asked. 'How would it look in court or out in the street if I cried for my clients, or for the poor of Calcutta? You want me to go and be a missionary,' he shouted finally. 'Or give our house to monks so they can take in lepers. You'd like to see me kiss their sores? Well? Would you? Would you?'

'Sometimes, Ewan McCarthy, you can seem dead to the world,' she said.

'Why do you stay with me then?' he asked, not really raging but cross-examining her, which drove her wild.

'Because we have come this far,' she said. 'Because I have faith in you.'

27 Sing Sweet the 'Marseillaise'

All this of course is gone now. Events lived in the searing present so quickly cool to artefacts and litter. Scars on the smooth tissue of the brain.

We are on the fields above St Agnes in the moment that is the now of Ewan McCarthy's long life. Ewan is cold from the previous hour's sweat and from the rain that has stopped, although the air is still heavy and sweet with moisture. You can see him? Reach out and Ewan McCarthy will surely acknowledge you. Six feet tall and sore in the back. Old clothes, jeans and a fisherman's sweater, breathing deeply and well, and the same face that has warned people off the scent so well for forty years. Ah, Ewan, the cat is out of the bag now. Tomorrow more men will come with deliveries, from out of town. Who from St Agnes, after all, would agree to work for Ewan McCarthy these days? Tomorrow sees the erection (now that the levelling is almost complete) of the construction cradle – the scaffold within which he and Salazar will then build the ark in accordance with the wishes of the Brooklyn GI conscript of 1944, Sol Werbernuik.

And then Ewan begins to sing. Shy and faltering. Not so much as to be ashamed, but hesitant and barely hopeful. On Mahoney's damp fields above the town Ewan McCarthy sings the opening bars of the 'Marseillaise' in his square-syllabled and self-conscious French. If anyone down in the town hears, they will think only that it is Ewan McCarthy, the madman. His poor wife, they will say.

There have been two worlds inhabited by Ewan McCarthy. Two ways of seeing things which have sometimes been thought of by him as being first innocence and then experience. But only now it seems has the world of experience – of things hard and eager – been overthrown and innocence won through. And so, leant against Pennine rain, the single word 'teva' scarred into the earth beside him, Ewan McCarthy, balding now, happy to be sure, anxious to set the foundation for the construction cradle, digs.

28   Here Stands Ewan McCarthy

In Mahoney's Wood, the clumps of wild and optimistic daffodil were giving way to meadowsweet and to trees in bud eager to press on and to the scents of new life lying clotted over the ground, and Ewan McCarthy, ten and with the seriousness of Solomon, walked up through the fields to camp with conviction in his heart for today was the day of the World Series. So many years later he is still there, still walking. Can't you see? Ewan McCarthy, ever the novice hitter, nervousness like sludge in his belly and a seed of greatness in his tremulous heart. The childhood we had is so close at hand, so close. Only by stamping down on the shoots of memory do we hope to make an escape, but there is no escape. We stay captive to those dreams, those demons in the dark, those ghosts. Whatever befalls us, we remain children – children simply wearing long pants and carrying histories; children wishing, pleading to be someone other, somewhere else, somehow grown and different, somehow complete, children knowing in secret ways how far we have fallen short.

There had been other days like this. Days remembering Sol Werbernuik's voyages. Days up by the observation point above the town or sat in the café while cool rain fogged the windows and shrunk the day until it fit the size of the table-top they sat around and Sol Werbernuik, spectacles moist like the window, drew maps. Some days, when the Arkin girl was sick or when the café was busy with Yanks, Sol Werbernuik helped out with the cooking in the kitchen since he had joined the army as a mess cook and had only transferred later to be a rifleman.

'So why'd you become a rifleman?'

'Well, Nick Adams, maybe I had it to do.' But there were other honourable trades in war as well as fighting, he said. Walt Whitman had worked in an infirmary dressing men's wounds. Hemingway had been an ambulance driver in Italy. Sol Werbernuik had picked up enough on the boats that went out for three days to fish off Cape Breton to be a cook. The radio played and the café hummed and Ewan watched him through the hatch in his khaki T-shirt, and Ewan wondered if his mother's heart might some day be melted by Sol Werbernuik.

Then there were the stories. A child's ability to be somewhere is not a physical thing but is ordained by love and by fear. There had been fear when they had broached Lancaster Sound and the polar bear (half an elephant's length and with that serpent's head) had hauled itself – slow motion hydraulics – out of the water onto the ice floe, noticed them sourly, then slipped back down into the water on the other side and away, with Ewan still waiting for the splash. There had been slow days securing lobster pots. There had been wide and sprawling days filled by two thousand musk oxen on the silent plain above Jameson Land. There had been rowdiness and craftsmanship in the boatyards of Maine.

They hunted rabbits in the woods, Ewan scouting and hissing 'There, there' and Sol shooting and the two of them laughing at how the rabbit got away. They set up camp for Ewan to sleep out in the woods one night. Sol Werbernuik rigged up canvas sheeting and a blanket. It was a long night and Ewan heard noises. Though he could see the lights of the small town below, he was astonished at how desolate and estranged a traveller he felt. He slept fitfully, waking with his shoulder and his leg aching despite the hip trench the soldier had dug for him. Noises scared him. He had the dream again. And in the morning Sol Werbernuik came and they ate chocolate and drank water from Sol Werbernuik's hip flask while Ewan told him how it had been, and the two blood brothers rolled the damp canvas up together and left for the town.

'What kind of man will you be?' the soldier asked.

Sometimes Sol Werbernuik spoke about things which the boy couldn't grasp. Sometimes he had ideas about things which Ewan knew were the first time they had been thought of in that way, and talking of them was like making tracks in clean snow. Sometimes Sol Werbernuik made notes of things, and now and then he let Ewan see.

'I'll be like you,' the boy said.

'Don't be like me,' Sol Werbernuik said.

'Why not?'

'Because.'

Another time, the soldier said, 'Don't be left with things to say. Be like Hemingway or Walt Whitman. All of them used up and necessary in what they do and the last drops squeezed out of them. Be like Mark Twain – write "Here Stands Ewan McCarthy" on all your days.'

29 Planning for the Future

After a while it became difficult to remember clearly a time when the Americans had not been here, at least for Ewan, and so he surmised for others. The war itself had lasted more years than memory reliably stretched. The war was a permanent feature and people were foolish to anticipate its end, Ewan McCarthy realised, though this secret was a jewel he kept clutched to his own pale white chest.

The Americans at the camp had surely forgotten whether they had ever once come from other places for their home was here now, perched above St Agnes – strong men who knew how and when to smile unashamedly, come to play their part in the pageant of St Agnes' life. They were here and it was best if everyone accepted it. Lampeter's sister had accepted it, eager as she was herself to press on with life. She was engaged now to a Canadian called Johnny whose company was stationed in a derelict mill in Euxton but who came some weekends into town to drink at the Tavern where they'd been taught how to drink Guinness and to sing 'The Quartermaster's Stores' and where, sporadically, Canadians fought fistfights with Americans and one time fought with the Americans against three Negroes from a black unit who'd tried to buy drinks at the Tavern.

Ewan learned about the Canadian from Lampeter's notes. The two boys hadn't seen each other lately – Ewan was, after all, blood brother to a soldier – but every few days he got a letter in Lampeter's precise and cautious script. ('I have found out that it was King Zog who ruled Albania after C. B. Fry had declined the throne.')

Lampeter wrote to Ewan that his father was sending him to public school in Lytham when he had recovered. His father, Felix Sommer, Alderman and businessman, had the money of course. Felix Sommer went around feeling cheated, sold short that Lampeter wasn't a sporting kind of son, that Lampeter wasn't so big and athletic as to dominate those around him physically, which is what Felix would have liked for his son to be. His compensation, such as it was, was that Lampeter was studious and clever and had good manners. Felix Sommer was impatient for Lampeter's recovery so that the boy could go away to school and make good friends (he called them contacts), and when he was older could run the business empire in the town with his father when the damned Yanks had gone. Felix Sommer loved his daughter, on the other hand, for being an ornament and a flirt with him, and he would have paid well to have any man broken who touched her. He seemed to know so little about her. Lampeter's mother, a quiet woman penned in still further by her husband's need to command each social situation he encountered, was easier with Lampeter's reticence and sense of promise than with the flibbertigibbet daughter she had borne. It was a preference which Lampeter's patient and unremitting illness had served only to accentuate. Lampeter was no bother, his mother told people. But that other madam . . . there were not the words, and she would say it not with speech but with her eyes and the other women on the street understood in a way that Felix Sommer didn't. When Lampeter was grown, she said, he would go to university and read medicine and would walk arm in arm with her round the college quadrangle. Lampeter knew none of this.

The future had become a seductive and untrustworthy ally. When people looked down that long St Agnes Roman road and saw the bombing of Manchester as a red glow on the cut of the horizon, when they queued for two hours on the loosest of rumours that this or that shop had apples, when men came home on leave striving to have a year's life in a weekend or else slumped by the radio asking for nothing, then the future became mistress to the marriages people had formed with the here and now of war – bizarre, improbable, necessary and plaintive scripts.

Ewan McCarthy's life, by contrast, offered a seamless transition into what lay ahead. Ewan and Sol Werbernuik would make their livelihood together and leave new tracks in snow freshly fallen. Elsewhere people would have won the war and seen Hitler tossed into the same eternal pit in which Horace Weir was captive and where both of them would be made to stand naked and be laughed at as retribution from the world of good men.

The field beyond the staked-out army camp behind the bunk tents was warm from the sun and right for baseball. This field was maybe three hundred yards square, its turf flattened to the scalp of the earth, and here and there men were scattered about in conversation, one group throwing a ball about and horsing around the way men do in sunshine after winter has been on their backs for so long.

The secret of baseball, Sol Werbernuik said, was the rhythms it contained. Punctuation was important because it built the tension and turned things into celebration. So the two of them took care to select the best part of the field and to measure out the four bases carefully in strides. They worked the position of the bases so that a yew tree on the edge of the field filled the backstop position behind the plate. Sol Werbernuik drew a rectangle on the bark of the tree with chalk.

'You gotta pitch in that area when I'm batting,' he told Ewan. Then they sat down and inspected their baseball field. They knew the World Series could not begin till four o'clock. Sol Werbenuik had said so. It was warm so they sat down.

'Can I look at the bat?' Ewan asked.

'Sure you can, Nick Adams,' Sol Werbernuik said. 'Hold it. Swing it. Get the feel of it, the balance. How its weight takes you with it.' He drew the baseball bat from the canvas case in which he carried it. It was a pale wood, and smooth as onyx, with the finest of grain lines etched over the surface, lines like veins that might have brought it life and sustained it. Ewan took the bat and was surprised by its weight, but when he stood up and held it at the grip with both hands it lost maybe half the weight he had felt initially and the bat swung back and forth in his hands with more grace than he himself knew how to give it.

'That's good,' Sol Werbernuik said. 'That's real good. Now, you need to imagine striking the ball. This bat, like all true bats, has a sweet spot which, if you catch it, will smack the ball with such a song that you would not believe it possible.'

Ewan held up the bat again for inspection, one hand at either end, and again the dull weight returned to it as soon as he surrendered the proper grip.

'Is this your bat? Your own, I mean?'

'This bat was originally my uncle's,' Sol Werbernuik said, pushing the wire-rimmed glasses back onto the bridge of his nose. 'Jonas Werbernuik was not a man who won so much or for whom things went right too often, although he did come to play baseball in the semi-pros and to use this bat. When he retired he took to baking bread for a living which is how he brought me up after my parents died, and how I came to take up the kind of life I did when I was fifteen. And so now I have the bat. I wrote a story setting out how Jonas, my uncle, came to play semi-pro, and after the war is over I hope to have the story published.'

'Who will publish it?' Ewan asked.

'Oh, I think maybe the *New Yorker* or some such magazine. They are always on the lookout for new writing talent and I think this will be the kind of story that they would be interested in publishing.'

Ewan held the bat at the grip again and this time tried to imagine, as he swung gently, the crack of the wood hitting the ball and having the ball sing out over the field. When Ewan looked round, Sol Werbernuik had sat himself down close to the yew and was lighting a cigarette in the cup of his hands.

'Do you have the things you've written with you, here?' Ewan asked. The bat swung to and fro in his hands. Sol Werbernuik blew out the first drag of the cigarette and pushed the packet back into the breast pocket of his uniform.

'When I finish a story or some other piece of writing which I might one day use in a novel,' Sol Werbernuik said, 'then I send it back home for safe-keeping to a post office box number in New Jersey I have. War is no place to go carrying treasure around. And the thing about treasure, as all pirates who have ever buried it knew – treasure like gold or jewels or stories to be published which will make your fortune and your reputation – is the sure knowledge that when you finally go back you will dig it up with the promise that this treasure will provide you with everything you will ever need to survive in the world from then on.'

'Will you tell me about your uncle?' Ewan asked. 'About what you say in the story that you'll get published when the war is over?'.

'Jonas?' He smoked the cigarette and seemed to think about it, then set down for Ewan McCarthy the nuts and bolts of the story he had written based on his uncle's life, for there was still plenty of time in hand before the first pitch of the World Series on the fields above Mahoney's Wood.

31 Jonas Werbernuik

Jonas Werbernuik was six foot ten though he knew himself to be small under the stars. People thought Jonas's fear of them was gentleness. He walked with a slow bob and a rise, bob and a rise, like his body was stiffly hinged and his back unduly laboured. He was a small-town giraffe with a stammer and a tic. He was so clumsy off the field. So fish-out-of-water kind of clumsy. Things happened around him.

Jonas Werbernuik was the tallest high schooler in the long history of the county but somehow it didn't seem enough. He broke the school pitching record and travelled hopefully on a Greyhound to Galleon, Michigan with an overnight bag and a contract for a trial season with the Galleon City Mariners in his pocket. He'd find a six foot six wife and settle down in a neat old house and throw the ball with such a whiplash precision and so on and so forth.

Baseball was a beautiful game, he knew. It deplored contact (and Jonas was a giraffe not made for contact) and required grace, yet it demanded a physical commitment. Jonas was happy to show commitment on the island field. More than once this game had saved him from despair. More than once this game had sung of hope in his overripe heart. Jonas thought of baseball as lyricism for the tongue-tied poet. Maybe he would say that when he made the Hall of Fame. Jonas Werbernuik was born to pitch balls with that peculiar torque of his. Six foot ten and stiffly hinged and with occasional pains in his back like his body was crying out that this was all too much, too much. Lord knows, he seemed suitable for little else in this world.

At school he wasn't so bright. He never made the school debating team, didn't run for class president. Some wise guy, probably Tommy Schaeffer, voted him the boy most likely to skip class reunions. Around town (the place had been named Sacred Heart by its founders but someone at the state registry in Jefferson's day got the 'a' and the 'c' the wrong way round), waiting for manhood and the story to unfold, Jonas had stuff to remember. Going through doorways, he had to remember to duck. Opening his mouth to speak, he had to remember to wait until he'd got hold of a hard, pure snatch of air and to sing the words out.

'Hey, Werbernuik, you on the field Friday night against Hartford?' Tommy Schaeffer, who batted first and in the football season played running back, might ask.

'I sure hope I am,' Jonas might take a crack at singing, and sure enough at some point he'd . . .

'Screw you, jackass, I ain't got all day.'

. . . reach the end.

Ah me.

Pitching the ball, though, was all rhythm and the small chill of adrenalin, like ice on a hot day's skin, which came from being good. Baseball was truly the only thing he was any good at. Any use for. People told him so, though they needn't have bothered because Jonas knew. Jonas knew all along how much was riding on his striking out batters with that gift of his. His mother watched him carry his stupid, folded shape around the house, though if she ever watched him play – seeing the ball thrown from the arc of his pivoting shoulder – her physical sigh was not from the fear of him striking out as from relief that the gift remained.

It's Saturday – the morning after Scared Heart have won the championship game and Jonas, winning-team man, has headed into town. He has an errand. Jonas lives with his mom in a small farmstead on the edge of town. One day he's going to repay her for her nurturing an alien giraffe but for now his job is to sell the pick-up truck at Schaeffer's for the best price he can get. If they can get a hundred and fifty dollars Mom figures it'll cover the next quarter's mortgage payment on the fields till the harvest comes in. Make a good deal, she's said. Those fields are all we've got to help us up a little – unless you've got some plan of your own up there. She means up in his head, so far off the ground. She tinkles a laugh and Jonas cannot look at her for a moment, believing himself caught out for having plans.

'My mom said I was to ask for one fifty,' Jonas sought to explain.

'Hell, boy, you sure aren't built for haggling,' Schaeffer had said and offered him ninety dollars one final time, grinning and winning, grinning like he knew he had it in the bag.

Now Jonas drinks malt in the store across the street with ninety dollars rolled in a bundle in the pocket pressed to his heart. A man who has been watching him gets up and leans across his table and says, 'Excuse me, but you look like the kind of sleek giraffe who might have played last night in the championship match all the kids are talking about?' Jonas said he was and the man said he remembered, he remembered now so clearly.

97

The man is Pete Salinger. He is a freelance scout for the Galleon City Mariners as well as trucking for the Furry Cat Pet Food Company since the Mariners are not a wealthy team, semi-pro and on hard times. Pete Salinger pulls a contract of sorts from his pocket. Last night after the game, he explains, he wired Galleon and got permission to sign up the star pitcher who turns out to be Jonas Werbernuik on a trial contract to the end of the season. The only problem is the shortness of the deadline – signed contracts must be registered by this weekend or new players are ineligible until next season and by then, who knows, things might have passed them by. And since the contract needed to be registered by a certified lawyer it's going to come to maybe forty-five, forty-eight dollars in contract fees and lawyers' fees and indemnities and the like which Pete himself doesn't have on him and which would all be reclaimable once Jonas had made it safely to the Mariners over the weekend.

And so Jonas makes ready to pack an overnight bag and to take a chance in this one-chance world and to leave a note for his mom on the kitchen table.

'Dear Mom,' the letter started.

She kind of knew the rest and when her paper-thin heart gave out the next day as she stood in Schaeffer's place in town, who's to say it wasn't Jonas broke her heart?

'What happened to Jonas?' Ewan asked. 'Did he get to Galleon?'

But Sol Werbernuik said that this was enough for one warm afternoon and that he would doze a little until it was time to play and would finish off how Jonas 'the Giraffe' dealt with the world another time. And as Sol Werbernuik dozed off, bit by bit, in the field above St Agnes Ewan noticed that he did so with his arms clutched across his chest and that he looked so peaceful, like an angel. Only later, much later, years later, sitting drinking coffee in the dining room alone one night and listening to the piano playing of poor Thelonius Monk, who played with limping fingers and a sad kind of longing, did Ewan suddenly see how it was wrong for him, as Sol Werbernuik dozed, to have taken up the casual invitation of the loud men throwing the ball around across the field and to take a few strikes with Jonas's bat, but at the time it seemed so natural a boy's thing to do.

Ewan slipped the bat from out of Sol Werbernuik's canvas bag – Sol Werbernuik still slept and the sun shone – and joined the men who nudged each other and grinned and encouraged the kid to beat the ball to blazes. Each time he missed they whooped and hollered and sympathised with him and said to try harder this time round, but the bat was heavy and unwieldy in Ewan's hands and the sun seemed too warm to concentrate, and the ball too fast. And then Ewan noticed Sol Werbernuik stirring across the field and saw him catch sight of what was happening and sit up slowly, coming to, and Indian Joe pitched one final ball and Ewan suddenly knew that he had to strike this last ball cleanly out of the field for Sol Werbernuik's sake and for Jonas on that bus to Galleon. The ball thrown by the laughing Indian Joe curved towards him low and Ewan caught it full at the downbeat of the swing. The ball struck the wood with a smack and for a while it seemed that it must be a home run and fly beyond the field and over the wire of the fence, but at the last moment all the magic there was in it fell away and it seemed to sigh and died and fell short to the earth.

32   After Hours

It never occurred to Ewan as a boy to wonder why a man like Jacob Seebohm should conceive of founding a zoo in a quiet town like St Agnes, not a seaside town or a city with tourists or on the route to anywhere. It didn't strike him as odd for a man in his fifties to have done such a thing – a man who all his life had been in business, the fifth generation of a family of Sudeten Jews exporting smelted goods through Hamburg and Copenhagen and using old family connections to build a thriving trade in Europe and fill the pockets of St Agnetians with steady wages, a man without any previous interest in animals. Ewan knew only half the story but felt he had enough to get by on. Ewan did know that old Seebohm, whom no one in St Agnes saw much any more, had bought up the five-acre farmstead bordering the Seebohm estate outside St Agnes in 1921 and set about establishing the Seebohm Zoological Garden which opened to the public two years later. Ewan knew that in the aftermath of war and its absurdities and in the numbness of peace it was a fine place in which to be apart from things. Ewan knew that he could hide within the zoo grounds till all the day's visitors had gone and have the place to himself until the café across town on the

Padiham road shut at nine and his mother locked up and came home with the leavings tray they'd have for supper. What else was there to know? Sometimes things could seem sufficient in their incompleteness.

The shed at the back of the capybara pen was used for food-stuffs and for forks and hoses and the like. It was pinned through the hasp and staple by a padlock but Ewan McCarthy had discovered as he stood watching the capybara on what seems in memory to have been VE day – though he is sure he cannot have been left to wander on such a day as that – that the padlock didn't snap shut. The keepers only ever positioned the latch to trap the door in place. So Ewan, eleven now, watching capybara munching grass on VE day, hit upon a plan and that night hid away in the shed, behind bran sacks piled six high, as the last bell sounded for visitors to leave. After an hour the sound of keepers shuffling by died down and Ewan emerged.

That first evening his heart beat fast, waiting to be leapt upon (not by animals but men), but everyone was celebrating that the war was won. After that, two or three times a week Ewan hid away in the shed and emerged to spend the evening at the zoo alone and became gradually less edgy and more a part of things which was how he wanted it.

In the evenings herons came and nested on the elephant house. Badgers dug on the bank beside the capybara. Fox cubs played tag on the picnic lawn and shadows grew. One time in that victory summer Ewan watched from the goat mountain as the penguins on the far side of the zoo, maybe with a premonition of death, made an escape and were finally rounded up six hundred yards beyond the zoo grounds and galloping madly.

When finally Ewan himself was caught it didn't matter. At least that's how it seemed.

'Why the heck were you here?' the keeper asked. 'Don't you know you're supposed to leave when the last bell sounds? Have you been doing anything to the animals?'

'It's my zoo,' was all that Ewan would say, no matter what the threat. 'You leave me be.'

His mother's response was peculiarly indifferent when Ewan was escorted to the café.

'Do you know that it's wrong to trespass?' she asked Ewan.

'I suppose so,' Ewan said.

She turned to the constable. 'There,' she said. 'Are you satisfied now?' wrong-footing him hopelessly.

On his third capture by the zoo authorities Ewan was cautioned formally for trespass at the police station and his mother was called, and who knows where it might have ended had Ewan not soon after that run into Jacob Seebohm.

33   The Souls of Capybara, Too

Ewan knew there was another trespasser who frequented the zoo after hours as he did. Unlike Ewan, the second intruder never came to the zoo during the day, at least Ewan never spotted him. This other trespasser only appeared, like the herons, once the visiting public had gone home. He was a small grey man with a hat and an undistinguished coat and had he not been the only other human walking the grounds he would have been invisible to Ewan.

They walked into each other round one tight, priveted bend at eight o'clock on a fading spring night in 1946. Jacob Seebohm carried an umbrella. Ewan talked to him. After a while he confided about the capybara shed. Jacob Seebohm in his rasping woman's voice told Ewan about the spectacled bear he'd just accepted for the zoo and they watched it sleeping down in the vacant penguin pit. Stupid bear, Jacob Seebohm said. Most animals came to and lived their lives after the last bell, but this one . . . pthah! He made a gesture with his hand which Ewan didn't recognise. Ewan said that when he was older he'd earn a living writing about baseball and polar bears and love, and when Seebohm laughed Ewan feared that perhaps the old man was out to trap him. Ewan defended the spectacled bear's right to sleep in the evening after it had spent the day performing to people. Later, Jacob Seebohm offered Ewan the chance to help out in the evenings and at weekends at the zoo. That was how it came about.

When Jacob Seebohm, managing director of the Seebohm Plant, was interned in 1916 it came as no great surprise to St Agnetians since it was well known he'd been aiding and abetting the German war effort by trading with the Kaiser's men for years. They said so in their set square tradesmen's sentences and in their quicker looks and smiles than ran like water over and between their words. Not only that, but cousins of Seebohm with whom he'd corresponded openly until the outbreak of war (and then most likely by covert means) were fighting in the imperial army. When Jacob Seebohm was released fourteen months later people had come to expect that too, since it was clear by then that he was nothing more than a fifth-generation Jewish businessman who was unlucky enough to still have family and trade abroad. He came back one quiet morning by train from the camp near Carlisle where he had been interned. He walked up the High Street and people watched from their windows and noted that old Jacob was back. As he approached the Plant the women working there hurried out one by one and in the courtyard sang 'For He's a Jolly Good Fellow' and some cried and one or two hugged him and they all trooped back inside so relieved to have old Jacob back and to be thus exonerated by his return.

But it could never be the same when five generations of Seebohm patronage had counted for nothing. Nor could it be forgotten, no matter how folk tried, that on the morning Jacob Seebohm had been led away the workers had enjoyed a fine time singing 'Boiled Beef and Carrots', and that production was up in that month when all the nuts and bolts were counted as if to celebrate the spy's demise and the saving of the town by its inhabitants, and that someone had hung a banner across the street.

The first person Jacob Seebohm talked to about the internment camp – the first person who asked – was the doctor in Gstaad. No one in St Agnes could bring himself to mention it. The way they formed their sentences didn't lend itself to the task. It was, St Agnetians felt, an incident best forgotten.

'I was a spy,' Seebohm told the doctor, 'a spy and a traitor.'

'Do you believe this?' the doctor asked.

'What I believe does not count,' Seebohm said. 'What other people believe is what counts. This is what I have come to accept. No matter what I do, I am helpless to change the welter of people's ignorance, people who walk around with my money in their pockets and live on my sickness pay when they are ill and clap at concerts on Saturday evenings in the Civic Hall renovated by the charitable fund run by five generations of Seebohms.'

'How does that make you feel?' the doctor asked. 'Are you sad or angry or what is the emotion you feel?'

'I feel nothing,' Jacob Seebohm said. 'I am no longer a living person. I am a figment of other people's imaginary lives, a puppet to do with as they please.'

'What will you do, now that you cannot believe in people and now that they do not believe in the person who is you?' the doctor asked.

'I had better find something else to believe in,' Jacob Seebohm, fifty-two years old and in a strange land, said. 'That strikes me after all as the way of the world.'

Jacob Seebohm stayed at the clinic in Gstaad for eleven months. With his loss of interest in the Plant he had helped prosper further (he finally sold his shares in 1921), without his stewardship and with the absence of the drip-feed of war, the Plant was never as strong as it had been under Jacob. The other members of the family struggled on and made bad decisions. Then the Depression hit and St Agnes caught a whiff of bad times. Someone said they saw Horace Weir's bear close by the town but when a group of men went out with guns to see, they found nothing. Then, with war looming again, the Government offered to buy up the Plant from the remaining Seebohm clan and, other than a cut in sick pay and some retraining, the people of St Agnes barely noticed the change.

'Do you think animals are men?' Ewan asked him.

They were still standing watching the spectacled bear down in the penguin pit in the evening zoo emptied of people.

'I believe,' Jacob Seebohm said, 'that when men die, their souls are transmuted into the shapes of animals as penance for their lives. This spectacled bear, for example, was undoubtedly a St Agnetian before he died. You can tell it in his eyes and in the way he refuses to believe there is more to learn than the crumbs of knowledge he has foraged from the dirt and from his ridiculous owner who left him tethered to a lamp-post.'

'So you think the souls of bears and lions are men?' Ewan asked. 'And the souls of capybara, too?'

Jacob Seebohm nodded. 'My zoo is run with that philosophy in mind. All my animals are treated well because they were once, and will be again, people. But it is their turn now to be defenceless and relatively taciturn and vulnerable because of their previous sins, and it is my privilege and my responsibility to spend my money sustaining them in this condition until, God willing, they are ready to resume a human life somewhere, this time having learned things from their captivity. And in return the animals are grateful and that makes me happy. My responsibility is to these poor souls now.'

'Some people in St Agnes said you were crackers,' Ewan said. 'You go spending all your money on animals and you think daft things.'

'Then those people, if they're dead now, might well be here, might well be one of the capybara or a goat,' Jacob Seebohm – well into his seventies now and more or less content with the pact he'd made with life – said, and smiled, for the doctor in Gstaad had persuaded him of the value to his own soul of a smile or two peppering his days.

34   Old Scars

'So what happened?' Harris Leary said.

'The fucking macaque bit me.'

Ewan showed him the hand where, ten years later, the welt of an old scar still crossed his knuckle.

They were walking back from the magistrates court through the town, files in their hands, young men with shirtsleeves rolled to the elbow and jackets over their shoulders. Harris Leary's female client of seventy-three had been assaulted by a sixty-seven-year-old man who had brought her back to his flat for tea. Ewan had spent part of the morning defending a man who, over a two-year period, had stolen eighty-six books from the town's libraries on business and tax accountancy and two, by accident, on taxidermy.

'You strangled it?'

'Don't say it like that.'

'Like what? I never met a monkey strangler before.'

'God, I was so incensed. I nearly lost the finger. They took me to hospital with blood seeping everywhere. They said I could easily have lost it.'

Ewan had been bitten four months into his National Service, on his first visit home. His revenge on the macaque took place the next time he was on home leave from Catterick Camp, three months later when the wound itself was all but healed. I suppose you might say he planned it. Well, he was stupid still, and young, and hadn't quite got on top of life and beaten it to a shape he was happy with. He felt it was something that needed to be done. At the time it seemed to be his rite of passage into the harder world all about him. Boy, how the lads back at the camp had laughed when he told them the tale of how the monkey had bit him so he strangled it right back. Jacob Seebohm hadn't laughed, although at the time this seemed to be a small price to pay for Ewan's popularity with the thirteen good fellows around him in the hut on Catterick moor.

Those months he was back at camp after being bitten and before he had wreaked his revenge, not having too great a time of it, cramped up and folded into all those other lives, taking orders, having Libberman fall apart in the next bunk, having men bump and bang into each other's private days, into his own, day in day out, being mired in the crowd, he'd kept seeing this damned monkey at old Seebohm's zoo whilst his hand was all stitched up and throbbing like hell, and the monkey with that stupid grin like it had got the better of him and he kept thinking about Seebohm's thing that all the animals were really people, and that fucking macaque . . . intruding in on him like that.

Ewan touched the scar. 'It was so funny,' he said. 'The rest of the macaques stood watching, wondering what I would do next. .I felt so . . . released.' Ewan rubbed the scar again between the thumb and forefinger of his other hand but, no matter how much he touched it, the scar stayed ribbed on the raise of flesh across the knuckle and one inch down his finger towards the middle joint.

When the macaque stopped flailing in his hands and lay still, Ewan realised that he was cold and sweating. His arms ached. There was blood and hair on him. Something was lodged in his throat. Pieces of ligament like elastic were trapped under his nails. The macaque lay against him as if it were exhausted and not dead. He looked at his watch and saw that five or six minutes had passed, and he realised that he was unsure how much noise the monkey had made, whether he himself had made a sound, and whether it had travelled beyond the ape house. He looked around him. Slowly it dawned on him that he'd got away with it, that the other animals were not screaming with disgust or panic and no keepers were hurrying to the scene. Some of the monkeys were watching him. None accused him. They just got on with things. Curious. Hungry. Bored, scared, horny. He'd got away with it. He'd got away with it. Perhaps Seebohm was right and they were all former St Agnetians, dull, feeble as ever. No matter. No matter.

He had time before he left the ape house to stuff the macaque into a bran sack, then walked steadily across the yard toward the bin store, feeling as though he'd tested the rules at the edge of things and come away laughing.

When it was done it seemed a momentary aberration, a touch of comedy before his truer journey out into the world began, but the boys back in camp enjoyed the story and it seemed to even out the score and to gain him a certain reputation which he enhanced with stuff about the Americans and the way his mind could race faster than others to find words so he could appear to say what other men were thinking. Blacksmith's magic.

Of course Jacob Seebohm found out. Someone discovered the macaque wrapped in the bran sack in the bin. Pure chance. What upset Ewan most of all at the time was that Seebohm blamed him for the whole thing. Went on about the souls of men. Didn't seem to understand the monkey's role in all of this.

Pthah! Ewan couldn't calm him down and in the end (his knuckle still raw and aching some nights and him on guard duty until the hand had fully healed) he told Seebohm one or two home truths in a note he sent from camp. And that was pretty much the end of that.

35   Growing Pains

Mitch Murray's firm, like lots of outfits it was possible to come across in St Agnes, was a one-man business that got too big.

In the beginning it is easy for one man with energy and his name on the door to build a steady business employing four or five people and to take pleasure in ruling for himself on everything from the appointment of staff and work rotas to the colour of crockery and the range of biscuits to be stocked.

By the time Ewan McCarthy and latterly Harris Leary were signed up, the cracks were showing. By then it was an eight-man firm with all eight wishing for the day when their founding father was gone so they could turn things around to eight different prescriptions for success. It had a pooled secretariat and a loud, ramshackle man in his forties called Collins who wore prescription glasses and who had endured three marriages and who'd been with Mitch for years. Collins had an understanding, in return for money not always going through the books, to be something between a bookie's runner and a private investigator for the firm and whose speciality was serving injunctions in public houses. It was one of those subversive arrangements which was meant well but whose arbitrary nature upset everyone in the firm one way and another.

Mitch Murray, saint and saviour, charged clients all his life according to what they could pay based on a slide-rule system he kept in his head. Mitch had been known to move furniture, to rat-catch and to lend fivers whilst on duty. He welcomed each new employee to the firm like they were in-laws entering the family. He went as far as assuring each one that this was indeed a family firm. What he meant by that, though, was that as head of the household he felt he had licence to go poking in everybody's affairs, to make judgements without foundation, to assume that he was vital to some moving component of the business only to forget about it for three months before taking it up again with gusto.

Mitch Murray worked a fourteen-hour day. He always had. He couldn't sit still, and he smiled whenever he wasn't out of breath which wasn't so often. He ran the firm to his death as if no one was quite ready to run the case they were on and it sustained Ewan no end to strain against it. Harris Leary it merely entertained till things got serious, till he got into woman trouble.

The trick, of course, as Ewan soon discovered, was to be fast on your feet, to keep out of Mitch Murray's way whenever possible and when he did greet you – Ewan always felt like the prodigal being cornered by a beneficent father – to defer to him as though Mitch were the man who'd raised him from the dead.

Ewan McCarthy, man of the people, became so well-liked that, looking down one day from the heights he occupied, he realised that he feared nothing other than the resurrection of one mangy macaque.

It wasn't something that he could confess to too many people, of course. Small town life requires tact as well as a persistent kind of ability with people. He built an edifice slowly. He discovered pleasurably after some years that he was envied. He found a vantage point that helped him to see life in St Agnes as a scientist sees microbes on a slide or an aircraft pilot the conurbation of a city ten thousand feet below. He discovered, for example, that he could feel real sympathy for the criminals who provided him with a living. For swampmen, driven to their small acts by impatience and anonymity. But they needn't fear. Ewan McCarthy so often came to save them and, by accident, raised his own stature each time, with each small incident, little by little by little — an unavoidable by-product of a life more and more devoted to people and their ills. Would it be wrong of him to suggest that in the end he felt himself chosen? Special. Not just in the eyes of other men but by God. Of course it would. Hush, Ewan, hush.

36   Saints and Sinners

Winning business from the Seebohm Plant was the firm's big break. Until then, over half of the business time and lord knows how much energy was spent on Harris Leary's swampmen, lost souls who saw Mitch as perhaps an easy touch and brought in next to nothing to the coffers.

It was Harris Leary, still a junior in the firm, who came through with the goods. He played squash with a manager at the Plant called Loesser and got talking. The outcome some months later was the news that the Seebohm Plant were thinking of appointing a local firm to assist with the conveyancing work for the continuous influx of new employees as the Plant, now intent on producing Seebohm energy, grew and grew. The new men were scientists and technicians and managers and the like, and the Plant ran a policy of offsetting all the relocation expenses of such men and wanted to award the conveyancing to a local firm in a single contract. Mitch Murray despatched his three smartest dressers to go before him and negotiate. Mitch signed up and so the firm prospered and had spread across three facades and had won the leeway to continue servicing half the swampmen in town by the time Mitch Murray passed away and was mourned, his family apart, like a passing prince. Later, habit being what it was, Seebohm employees who had cause to feel aggrieved at the world or the Plant sometimes came back to Mitch Murray's firm to ask for representation. The partners of Murray Associates negotiated hard with the Plant and more often than not secured amicable arrangements that, as things turned out, had no need to reach open court. And year after year, the Seebohm Plant renewed its contract with Murray Associates to provide another year's conveyancing services for its workforce.

Harris Leary, who had reckoned himself half-way to partner, reckoned without Mitch Murray. Mitch, his finger in every pie, ruled that young Leary still had some humility to learn and where better to find humility than in nurturing swampmen through hard times. And so Harris Leary sought solace elsewhere. First he sought it with a couple of the secretaries. Then, rumour had it, with a client he was guiding through a divorce petition. Finally, he moved onto bigger fish and at that point became undone.

It was difficult later for Ewan to recall when exactly he first realised that Harris Leary had eyes for Ann. Harris Leary was so ridiculous and Ann was so sensible and level-headed about things that had Ewan caught the two of them holding hands, which he never did, he would have fished for a reasonable explanation. Besides, Harris Leary went for women with long legs and dirty minds – women who, he said, would fuck right through an earthquake.

It started with what seemed to be accidental meetings here and there. Ann was polite with him and Ewan was amused by the coincidence of these collisions. They always had the children in tow, of course, and Harris Leary would talk to them, amuse them, not show much interest in Ann from what Ewan could recall. Harris Leary had a trick with a penny and would make it disappear from his hand and reappear from inside the ears of the children, and they called him the 'Magic Man' and clapped and cheered when they caught sight of him in town which encouraged him further.

Then one time, with the firm's Christmas dance beckoning, Ann announced that she didn't want to go. Why not? Ewan wanted to know. She wouldn't say. Ewan got irritated.

'You complain that we don't get out enough together because of the children and the first chance for months you want to stay at home.'

'I don't want to stay at home,' Ann said. 'I just don't want to go to the dance. Let's go somewhere else, just me and you.'

'Don't be ridiculous,' Ewan said. 'What's Mitch Murray going to say if we don't go? You know what the bugger's like.

He'll take it personally and he'll spend the next month hanging round me looking for reasons for the slight against him.'

'I don't care. I just don't want to go.'

'Why, for Christ's sake, why? You want them to question my suitability for partner?'

'Because Harris Leary will be there.'

So she told him. She said that Harris Leary had started bumping into her more often. When she took the children to the park. When she went to town during the week. When she walked the dog. One time when she was collecting the kids from school. Always he said it was coincidence and always he was a perfect gentleman, never propositioned her or made a move. Finally she feared that he had started hanging round the house. She began watching from windows and sometimes she thought she could make him out down the street. Once she saw him for sure and ran out to confront him but he was gone when she reached the spot.

Ewan forced her hand and they went to the dance against Ann's wishes. Ewan had a sense that, if it was good to be quietly adept with people, it was better still to be seen to go dancing and the like. Work and play, Ewan. Work and play. Harris Leary wasn't at the dance, but then on Christmas Eve Ann revealed that he had been round, had come to see her at the house whilst Ewan was at work and said he was in love with her and said he dreamed about her nightly. He said he'd make a better husband than Ewan. He said that away from her he was bereft.

Ewan brooded on it over Christmas, wouldn't speak of it to Ann, then came back in after the break and sent a note in the post to Mitch Murray, unsigned, expressing disquiet at Harris Leary's pursuit of a colleague's wife. Though it rumbled on for a while — and Collins was somehow involved along the way — eventually, on grounds of breach of trust, although quietly since Mitch Murray liked things that way, Harris Leary was released from the firm. And so Ewan McCarthy prospered. With Harris Leary gone, purged, he settled down — found his feet Mitch Murray liked to say, although he never quite became the protégé Mitch Murray had fancied him to be. The manners, you see. Mitch had been fooled by those grammar-school manners.

One time Mitch was sat with him; the day was over and people were wrapping up and going. The town outside was clogged with laden shoppers and schoolchildren.

'What do you find to talk to your wife about?' Mitch asked him. People were walking past them as they spoke. Mitch didn't seem to mind. He assumed that everybody knew, or else would honour secrets.

'I find it so hard to talk to mine,' Mitch said. 'It's like trying to force a pee when it won't come.'

Ewan was embarrassed that Mitch Murray was talking to him like this, but felt certain that he'd hidden his awkwardness from the older man who was intent on his confession. Mitch said he slept poorly — it was mostly a medical thing. Every night he went to bed with his wife, only to wait for her to doze off when he crept downstairs and sat up until three or four in the morning drinking tea.

'What do you do?' Ewan asked.

'Do? Nothing. I just sit and think. Things keep me awake. Do they not you?'

Ewan shook his head, uncertain as to why he would want to own up to such things, how Mitch Murray could find life so perplexing.

Ewan remembered how Mitch had once lost his rag with him and with Harris Leary who was still at the firm then. On the wall of the office the two juniors had got into the habit of playing hangman. Each of them had a scaffold. Each time one of them lost a case in court they were compelled to add another line on the drawing. When finally one or other man was hanged he was added, drawn in full, at the end of a line of hanged men. At the end of the month the loser with the most hanged men had to pay for drinks. When Mitch Murray discovered it he called them both into his office.

'Its just for fun,' they said. 'What's the big deal?'

'No its not,' Mitch said. He spluttered and was ineffective the way he was in court – he was no great lawyer and everybody knew it. He was a better human being than a lawyer and even then, Harris Leary used to say, he wouldn't exactly have got an 'A'.

Mitch carried on confessing. He said his wife wanted to move house. Mitch had been trying to put her off for years. His kids, grown now, stumbled into troubles weekly. When he felt he ought to talk to his wife, no matter how he racked his brains and tried, nothing came. Nothing ever came.

When Mitch Murray sensed that he'd been duped and thought he saw proof that Ewan didn't love things – people – as unreservedly as he did, he made his observation, the one that echoed Jacob Seebohm's thought. It was inevitable after that, as Mitch got iller, that Ewan kept his head down. Ewan did at least tell stories which sang the praises of the man's legendary largesse since that was the currency of the day. It wasn't a case of being a hypocrite. Ewan McCarthy was doing what he did best – weaving a fine story of a goodish man whose passing would sadden everyone. He finally did turn up at Mitch's hospital bed to pay homage. By that stage he was virtually the last member of the firm to schedule a visit to the firm's dying founder and he refused to allow Ann to come with him.

'The state of him,' Ewan said. 'It wouldn't be fair on you.' In the fullness of time Ewan found he couldn't attend the funeral since he was out of town that day on business.

Mitch Murray had one final stunt to pull. Ewan discovered some weeks later that he had been summoned to the reading of the will. He mentioned it to Ann.

'You were his favourite at the firm, after all,' she said.

'I was not,' Ewan protested. 'I don't think he even liked me much.'

'He thought a lot of you,' she insisted. 'Maybe he wants to take this final chance to reward you for it.'

At the reading of the will the estate was split unevenly between Mitch Murray's family and the St Agnes Night Shelter, which didn't please everyone. Then they got down to the odds and sods. His car, a tank of a thing, an automatic he could barely see over the bonnet of; some paintings and the usual antique hand-me-downs; his flat in Corfu (he hated holidays, said he could never get the knack); his books; and so it went on.

'And to Ewan McCarthy, my trusted and admired young colleague, I leave something more precious and more necessary in this world than all of these things – my heart.'

People shook his hand, believing Ewan to be the recipient of the final blessing of a well-wisher, and when he came home empty-handed even Ann would only smile and refused to take his side, and the only consolation was the dog who, big lummox, sat by him all night knowing that every now and then Ewan would reach for him, as if for reassurance.

37 Love and Rhinos

Ewan McCarthy (weary footsoldier for truth) had Salazar (edgy) in his office. The building seemed logjammed. The shoplifter who had been rumbled in Debenhams and had fled the scene, abandoning her child, had been in court this morning begging Ewan for forgiveness. The man who had exposed himself in front of the ape house in Seebohm's zoo sat outside in the corridor waiting patiently to be seen. And so it went on.

Salazar had by now been put into group therapy by Jenny Aldred who herself was reported to be off work with shingles. Salazar was a jitterbug. He had been put on probation and given a suspended sentence for hitting the two policemen who had arrested him at the zoo. It was after that that he had been put in a group encounter programme. Things surfaced from him and popped and sizzled. The bear, Horace Weir's typhus bear, had cornered him, he would have Ewan believe. The bear had named a day when it and Salazar would have to fight in combat. Jenny Aldred was rumoured to be pleased with the progress made. She said it seemed as if the therapy might bring things to a head after all. To Ewan it looked like bloody chaos and he said as much.

'You're going to fight an imaginary bear?'

'I got to. Someone's got to fight the bear now that it has a taste for blood, now it's been back in the zoo and ripped them poor creatures to pieces. It'll be people next who'll be affected. That's how I think this thing will run unless I stop it.'

'Oh, fuck's sake, big man. I told you about that. It was people who did that at the zoo. Zoo people.'

Salazar smiled, all sympathy. 'Thanks for trying, boss, but I know people couldn't have done that. People aren't like that. Bears are like that. I know you're just trying to save me from taking on the creature and its good of you, but I have it to do. That's why I told the evening paper. They're going to write about it.'

'You've spoken to the local paper?'

Salazar nodded.

'Oh-aw Jesus Christ. Have you no sense? They'll just play you for a prat. Did you give them my name? What's Jenny going to say? God, you're a stupid man. Does Jenny know?'

'She's off. She's poorly, boss. You know she was crying last time I seen her. She said there wasn't anything I could do. I don't think she's so well in herself. Besides, I'm so busy now that the bear's around more and more. Its getting stronger. Braver. I tracked it to Jenny's flat. Sometimes it comes round your place when I'm doing the garden. I see it when it thinks I'm not looking.'

'Listen, big man, you don't go prowling round people's flats, bear or no bear. You forget about that bloody bear.'

'I wouldn't do Jenny no harm, boss. Not her. Not you.'

'I didn't . . . Oh, for Christ's sake,' Ewan started.

' . . . but that bear, I can't vouch for him. He's planning something. That's why I had to tell the paper about it.'

Ewan, seeing things starting to get out of hand, folded Salazar into his car and drove him to the zoo that lunchtime to show him the truth once and for all. He led Salazar to the courtyard which remained sealed off to the public. There, just as he'd promised, two men stood in the doorway of the outhouse cutting at the carcass of a half-grown rhino which had died the previous day. At first Ewan was relieved to see the wonder on Salazar's face, until he realised that his astonishment was not caused by seeing people hacking up animals in kitchen table post-mortems and putting the useless bits in bags to be shipped off to the dog food plant, but instead that Ewan loved him enough to have artificially manufactured the scene simply to persuade him that the bear wasn't the real killer.

As they walked back to the car Ewan suddenly said, 'You know the maple tree? The one below the patio? I want you to take the whole thing up. I'm worried about those roots. I can't get them out of my mind when I'm at work. I'm in court all day tomorrow and then I'm out of town most of Thursday, won't get back till seven or eight. When I get back on Thursday evening I want the tree up. You understand?'

'The whole thing?'

'It'll take two days I reckon, if you stick at it. Ann's down in Sussex with one of the boys. I'll leave the key for the back door in the toolshed so you can brew up. You okay with the dog?'

'There's other things I have to do. That bear, the other things.'

'Never mind the other things. You sort the maple out.'

Salazar agreed reluctantly to the two days' hard labour which would leave him no time for the other things, but maybe Ewan already suspected that such tricks were too late and that Horace Weir's bear already had too much of a hold.

The following day, the man who had shown his buttocks to the apes was given a suspended sentence and put on probation. On Thursday, Ewan travelled out of town to represent the Seebohm zoo in a series of meetings with creditors and a group who had expressed an interest in developing the five acres as a landfill site.

What reports survive of St Agnes in the 1730s show only that
the travelling preacher Horace Weir arrived on horseback
with a party of four, two women, a priest and a blackamoor,
and secured quarters for the night at the Wheatsheaf Hotel on
the High Street, booking three rooms. No one knew him, or
had seen him before, although a letter had arrived recently for
the Vicar of St Agnes Parish Church. The letter, sent from the
Bishop of Sutherland, suggested that a visiting dignitary would
be arriving and that the vicar would know the man by a sign
to be a friend in these difficult times. The vicar had not heard
before of the Bishop of Sutherland, although the quality of the
paper was excellent and the handwriting was scholarly, and
the gift of Madeira wine sent to the vicar from the Bishop and
conveyed by Horace Weir on that first night for the vicar's
labours during the months of typhus in St Agnes was a
welcome reward.

Perhaps the most unusual thing about Horace Weir's ca-
ravan was the very arrival of the little group itself. Everyone
in the country knew St Agnes had typhus. Boundary posts had
been erected as was the tradition, and sentries established on
all roads by neighbouring towns, and no one had left St Agnes
for four months prior to Horace Weir's arrival. And since no
one could leave, no one had entered.

It was this which explained the ease with which Horace
Weir drew a crowd the following day. Till then, letters in and

out had been nailed to a boundary post; sheep had been fenced in; travellers were signposted away until the infection had wreaked its full havoc and had finally passed.

Horace Weir, wearing a smock and with a crucifix around his neck, told St Agnetians that he had no fear of typhus or of death. He said that he had latterly returned from Palestine. He was, he explained, back in England as a disciple of the Church of Apostolic Truth having witnessed remarkable things in his time away. The Church of Apostolic Truth had been recently founded on the instruction of St Peter and St Paul, who had returned to Galilee these last months to complete their apostolic mission on earth. Whilst Horace Weir spoke, the two women and the blackamoor passed amongst the crowd distributing printed sheets setting out these events, although few could read well enough to understand them.

The citizens of St Agnes, Horace Weir said, had been denied the chance to rejoice with the rest of the world at the news of the return of Peter and Paul to their earthly ministry. Sickness had tested their resolve and their belief in a benevolent Father in Heaven and the proximity of last things. But now the good news was at hand. For only five shillings, the Church of Apostolic Truth could underwrite the entry of any repentant St Agnetian into Paradise on the Day of Judgement and would provide authentic certification to prove it. There was a special fee of only two shillings for anyone too far gone with sickness to hope for recovery. This was in order that even men dying this very week and without the time to sell livestock or property to raise sufficient capital could meet their Maker with the confidence of salvation in their hearts. And to confirm the majesty of the Church,

Horace Weir summoned up three large flashes and commanded that the Apostles in Heaven offer to St Agnetians any single thing which their good hearts most wished for and promptly turned the typhus epidemic into a bear. The bear, startled to be so transformed and limited by God, ran out of the smoke into the fields and beyond the boundary posts around the edge of town which now marked the edge not of sickness and death but of blessed, recovering quarantine.

At night, returning to the town through the hills, it could seem a special, jewelled place, wrapped with black and spread with lights. Ewan McCarthy, warm in the train, the rickety-rack of the wheels beating at the warm soles of his feet, was heading home. Another task, another safe return, another day. Ah life. The giant twin globes of the Seebohm Plant hung like moons beyond the town. The train started its puff-pull breaking sequence and Ewan waited for the station sign to slide into view and began looking for his car across in the car park. Cities grow in the night, but towns shrink into the older, medieval places they once were. Towns are simplified, made quirky and insubstantial by arrivals like this. Maybe it was a night like this when Horace Weir rode into town. Maybe Horace Weir saw the objects of people's lives here (to get rich, to pass through safely and without accident) thrown asunder, and people eager to revive some certainties and judgements. Maybe Horace Weir saw the town shrunken into the night and imagined families huddled and waiting for things to pass.

The station kiosk was still open and Ewan bought an evening paper. They had run the story Salazar had given them. The young reporter had worked hard to give it the right flavour and the editor had been happy enough with the result as a filler piece. 'MISSING BEAR STALKS LOCAL MAN CLAIM . . . Allegations that a fully-grown black bear has escaped undetected from the troubled Seebohm Zoo have been dismissed as bear-faced cheek by the zoo's authorities.

'The authorities dismiss suggestions that the bear story is a stunt designed to "panda" to public opinion and bring the failing zoo a last-minute surge of much-needed publicity. Just someone playing monkey business, they say.

'And keepers are denying that lax security as the zoo winds down might have made it possible for any animal to have given them the slip as at least one local man has suggested.'

In the last paragraph there was brief mention of Horace Weir, and of Salazar's claim that the bear was Horace Weir's, come back to signal bad portents for St Agnes as Weir had promised. 'Can it be,' the story ended, 'that Horace Weir's curse on the children of St Agnes is about to befall us? We don't know about you, readers, but it seems bear-ly credible to us here at the *Citizen*.'

Ewan drove home from the station, the evening paper folded on the passenger seat. The lights were out in the house. Ann still wasn't back. Ewan parked in the garage and, in the last of the light, went round the back to see how Salazar had fared with the maple. A crater was sunk four feet into the ground. Surface clay gave way half-way to black earth. It must have taken all of the day to dredge that much earth. Salazar had piled the soil and clay he had dug out into a flatter ridge running twenty feet over by the fence. The maple itself had been cut into logs that mostly lay stacked on the patio. Then Ewan saw the dog, and realised that all was not as it should be. Soil was scattered round the top lawn as if flung. Some branches the size of men's limbs lay out of place. Left in a hurry, maybe. Dropped. And the back door, when Ewan eventually tried it, was unlocked. The dog lay dead by the hole.

Ewan knelt down and lifted the dog to him. Its eyes were glassy. The skin around the neck was marked. Ewan rocked him back and forth and stroked the dog's head and put the pieces of the day together one by one and realised that Salazar had done this. Salazar, believing he was fighting the imaginary bear that stalked him, had done this, mistaking the dog in his lunatic head for the bear.

Ewan carried the dog to the shed, yielding under the weight, and covered him with a tarpaulin sheet. He secured the patio doors from the inside, then came out through the front door, locked up and brought the car out of the garage again. He drove slowly and, if you asked him later what he had thought of as he drove, he would not have been able to tell you. He felt a stillness in his head and his stomach heavy with grief and his hands tingling and his arms stiff as he drove. He felt some panic, and half-way there he realised that he had left no note for Ann who if she arrived home in the meantime, would be looking for him and the dog.

The social services centre was a single-storey building with most of the offices in darkness since it was gone eight-thirty. The entrance lights were on, as were those for the caretaker and the ones which lit the meeting room further down the corridor where Jenny Aldred's therapy group was nearing the end of its Thursday session.

Ewan knocked on the door twice and opened it. Nine or ten faces looked round. Salazar was there but Jenny Aldred, still sick, was not. In her place was a man Ewan didn't recognise, though Ewan didn't like him on sight. The man, though clearly not so old, had little hair and affected to have what was left cropped short to his skull. He wore fashionable big-rimmed glasses, that shrunk his eyes, and his hands were folded neatly in his lap so as not to allow his own body language to give things away. The poor sods in the room clearly hung on his every word and Ewan marked out Jenny Aldred's colleague or replacement as a shit and probably a supercilious shit to boot.

'Jenny isn't here?' Ewan asked, annoyed with himself that he was stating the obvious.

'No, no, she isn't,' the supercilious shit said. No one else said anything.

'I just wanted to speak to Salazar,' Ewan said.

Salazar caught his eye, then looked across to the shit.

'We'll be about fifteen minutes if you'll allow us to finish,' the shit said, emphasising his patience with the intrusion. Ewan looked back at Salazar, but the big man wouldn't look at him a second time and had his head bowed. Ewan noticed the woman sitting next to Salazar was white-faced and had been crying and then just as quickly saw that it was Mrs Heaney.

'It won't wait,' Ewan said. He was fully in the room now. 'If Salazar will come outside with me, the rest of them will be able to carry on in peace.'

'I am sorry,' the shit said, 'but I am going to have to ask you to allow us to finish the session.'

Ewan ignored him and turned to Salazar. 'I want to talk to you outside, now,' he said. Salazar kept his head down.

'I know you can hear me, so stop looking away. I've just been home and I've found the dog. I know what's happened.' Salazar still would not look at him but looked across instead at the shit.

The shit said, 'Salazar has been telling us about the dog. However, I feel it's important for his own well-being, and for the group as a whole, that you leave now and allow us to wrap things up properly as a group before you discuss things with him, outside the building, afterwards.'

'Discuss? I don't want to discuss. I want to know how the dog died.' He moved towards Salazar who, instinctively, stood up.

'Why'd you do it, big man? Eh? Why'd you kill the dog? Why'd you have to kill the only thing I had. Think it was the bear, did you? Think Horace Weir's lousy bear had come for you like you said it would. Except it wasn't the bear, was it? It was the dog. You thought the dog was your stupid fucking bear and you hit it with the spade after it came sniffing round you and you ran off when you saw what you'd done. And then you thought if you came here tonight for your weekly dose of feelgood grief and told the shit and all your goofy friends, then it would all be alright and everyone would forgive you.'

Ewan turned to the shit. 'So tell me, have you all forgiven him?' he said, and then to Salazar again, 'Do you feel better now your goofy friends have forgiven you?' Ewan still stood in front of Salazar who stood himself, hands down, head down, not looking at Ewan.

'Want to know something? I don't forgive you. I give you kindness and you kill my dog because you think it's a fucking bear that you made up in your head.' Ewan struck him in the face a first time and then a second.

'If you come near the house again I'll kill you,' Ewan said.

There was blood coming from Salazar's nose. Some of the women in the room were crying.

40 Throwing Dice

When the parcel arrived for Ewan at the firm's offices, he had almost forgotten about Rachel Tallow. The parcel contained a diary kept by her son, and several notebooks. There was also some family history which she had drawn out and which she thought he might find useful if he agreed to take the case further, and a handwritten note from her. Ewan left them piled on the filing cabinet by the window. These were not good days and he could do without distractions. He left them in his office for two days, then he read them through. That evening he called Rachel Tallow at home.

Salazar had rung the vet when he realised that he couldn't wake the dog which had died in its sleep – the phone number was pinned on the kitchen noticeboard beside the veterinary insurance card. Blind with panic and concern, Salazar had tried at first to pick up the animal and carry it but the weight of the dead dog after the day's digging and dredging and hacking at the maple was too much for him and he had caught the dog's head on the fence post and given up and had put the dog back down on the lawn and rung the number on the board. The vet confirmed the story when Ewan took the dog's body in for disposal the following morning.

'He was very upset about it when he rang,' the vet told Ewan. 'Your man I mean.'

'Yes', said Ewan. 'Yes.'

Ewan read the notebooks and the diary. The notebooks set out details of various incidents at the Seebohm Plant, including one in 1987 which differed from the Plant's own version, statements from other workers, and measurements which Rachel Tallow's son had contrived to take when he became suspicious of the Plant's safety record. The diary was a straight narrative of David Tallow's illness, showing how his body changed and became his enemy, became the weight that bore him down through his last nine months.

The records, sent as information to demonstrate that Rachel Tallow's direct family tree was previously clean of the leukaemia which killed her son, showed that Rachel Tallow had been adopted locally as a baby just after the war's end and was not the natural kin of her sister Helen who had died of the illness. The man registered as Rachel Tallow's father by her natural mother was Sol Wérbernuik, an American GI stationed in St Agnes during the war. The note asked Ewan simply to read the things she had sent him without obligation. She signed the note 'Rachel Tallow-Werbernuik'. The note said that she understood Ewan might have known her father during the war. She said to ring her after that if Ewan felt it was something he wanted to do. She said that she regarded this as her last throw of the dice.

41   Breathing Life

In five days they have built the wooden skeleton of their ark. Now, ribs rise and curve into the promised shape of the *Good Hope*. The belly of the boat rests on stilts set into the construction cradle which is dug into the earth. Salazar says it's like a Christmas turkey, flesh picked clean and the carcass bare to the elements. They laugh at that, and the sun heats their backs and they pull and tug at the tasks of the day. They fetch and carry planks, and the sound of nails striking firm wood carries through the afternoon. Ewan has plans and drawings unfurled on the wooden tool chest and weighted with stones. Once, they stop to drink beer from the bottle. Another time they lay down their tools as if prearranged and sit together on the grass and Ewan tells Salazar about the field, the camp, the yew which still grows by the edge of the field. Otherwise they work, as they have done for five days, breathing life into the carcass that will become a Newfoundland whaling boat.

42 The Worm in the Apple

There was a gap of eight days in the spring of 1944 – Ewan counted them – when he did not see Sol Werbernuik. Ewan had several thoughts about this. He thought it was possible that Sol Werbernuik was making arrangements for after the war. He believed Sol Werbernuik might be writing, needing privacy and the concentration of several days' solitude. There was the possibility that he was on jankers, for Sol Werbernuik, like Stolley, the salesman from Detroit, was a famously poor driller and marcher though he lacked the salesman's knack for avoiding the consequences. Of course there were other fears but it was best for blood brothers to allay them. It crossed Ewan's mind, for example, that the aborted World Series game would prove to have been the worm in the apple.

During this time Ewan received another note from Lampeter. It seemed somehow to be unexpected, and the thought of that cool room and the smells of Lampeter's recovering sickness led Ewan to decide to keep away a little longer, at least until Sol Werbernuik had reappeared and until Lampeter was a little stronger and able to emerge from his room for an hour or two. So Ewan stayed around the café. Plenty of Americans came and went but not Sol Werbernuik. Sometimes two or three of them came in the back way carrying boxes which they left in the kitchen, winking at the Arkin girl who watched them silently and offered them no encouragement. Ewan volunteered to help but was told 'no' matter-of-factly by his mother and so he stuck to playing double-handed pinochle the way Sol Werbernuik had taught him and working out his world cricket elevens based on different permutations of their Test Match records, but he got bogged down in the absence of his *Wisden*.

The news that Sol Werbernuik had been beaten up, and his appearance when he did eventually show up at the café, Ewan found reassuring. Cuts and bruises would heal. Sol Werbernuik's absence at least now had a tangible reason which made the absence safe and impermanent. It was the news which came after that, though, that Sol Werbernuik had been with a woman, which started the rot.

Ewan accepted the fact of the beating, and the reality of Sol Werbernuik's broken face, and for a few days things were as before. They played pinochle in the café and the Arkin girl brought them both lemonade in a pitcher and touched the bruises on Sol Werbernuik's face and laughed with them both about it. Ewan asked about Sol Werbernuik's stories, about Jonas and his gift, and Sol Werbernuik took up the tale for him as he remembered it written down and waiting for the war to end. 'I'll write about you as well,' Sol Werbernuik said. 'About the crash when the men died, and about the World Series game we'll have, and about the hunting in the woods.'

Ewan didn't ask about the fight and Sol Werbernuik didn't volunteer anything. The only sign that things were different was that Sol Werbernuik got up and left the café when Indian Joe and Stolley, the salesman from Detroit, and the two Bostonians who sometimes made deliveries round the back of the café turned up, and Ewan guessed that the fight had been with one of these. And when Sol Werbernuik had gone, the four Americans placed their orders with the Arkin girl and asked where Worm had gone, and told her that mess cooks couldn't ever be real soldiers and weren't real men either, they were likely as not faggots with no brains and no courage and scared of their own shadow, and the four of them ate what the café had in that day like they hadn't eaten for two days.

43 Ferrying Supplies

Supplies were always being trucked around town. With so much being shipped up to the camp, in and out of the Seebohm Plant, to and from the railway sidings, small quantities going astray wouldn't be missed and would hardly do

136

much harm and might do some good. Or so people reckoned. Thus men traded here and there, with each other and with the Americans. They traded foodstuffs, petrol, anything rationed and in short supply, and saw it not as a betrayal of the war effort but as a means of oiling the wheels of life in St Agnes secretly and without fuss, a kind of public service. Some men became adept at this game, became well-known and made money. Men like Felix Sommer and half of the Chamber of Commerce as it turned out. They were scornful of those further down the scale of things who ran the risk or were caught with a hundred cigarettes or in the act of syphoning petrol from an official vehicle while the driver fucked a local girl in the house on the corner.

Felix Sommer, owner of three butcher's shops in town and that Last Chance Café on the Padiham road, and Alderman of St Agnes, did a deal with Stolley, the salesman from Detroit, one night in the Tavern on the High Street. Felix Sommer, whose only wish was to make a better world for his boy by making money, did a deal involving the channelling of stock through the Last Chance Café, as though these were supplies the café was taking for itself. Some of these supplies were collected again by the Bostonians when the heat was off, sometimes by other men who Sylvie McCarthy and Ewan and the Arkin girl didn't know but were obliged to let in to rifle through the stock.

Felix Sommer wondered why folk should pay good money for Spam on the weekly six-ounce meat ration, or for Horlicks sweets or coffee like charcoal when they'd happily pay a little over the odds for better things, for tins of ham or fruit, or for ice-cream in quietly arranged barters. Better things, Alderman Felix Sommer knew, were stored in the mess stores on the hill and in the hangar of a depot over in Euxton than ran a thousand yards in length and from which all the US camps in north and east Lancashire were supplied. How much fuel lay laggardly in storage which could be of more use in the petrol tanks of people who needed it? How many better things could be had for the benefit of St Agnetians? How many cigarettes? How much whisky? How much food? Felix Sommer's philosophy, which he hoped Lampeter his son would take up, was that men who accrued wealth or position had done so as reward and so was a measure of virtue. Those who hadn't were less worthy and less to be trusted. Sometimes, in the café's pantries, boxes were left for days and appeared to have been forgotten in the hue and cry of things, and so Sylvie McCarthy took it upon herself to open them and used them here and there in what she cooked for the café – sometimes eggs, sometimes meat or sugar or oils. She charged nothing extra and she made no money. She disguised the food in casseroles and pies and the like. She did it for the satisfaction of making the meals as best she could. She never got caught and she took nourishment from the vague belief that she was doing her best. When the salesman from Detroit and Felix Sommer finally stumbled upon the fact that crates and boxes were going missing, they suspected Sol Werbernuik. He had declined to get involved with them, but had nevertheless aroused their suspicions by spending his days hanging around the café.

Sol Werbernuik hadn't seen the deals as Felix Sommer and the salesman from Detroit did. At least that was what he said. The salesman reckoned it to be cowardice. Whatever it was, Sol Werbernuik declined to get involved when the salesman offered him ten per cent of the proceeds to be made on whatever Sol would liberate from the mess stores whilst he was on guard duty. The salesman knew that those on guard rota at the mess stores had the greatest opportunity of anyone to salt goods away, and it was a great frustration that Sol Werbernuik wouldn't oblige him, since the others on the rota were too stupid or talkative or too greedy or hooked up to some other scam. Whatever – whether from pride or stubbornness or cowardice or something else, Sol Werbernuik told the salesman from Detroit to go hang.

Stolley, the salesman from Detroit, already employed two runners, Schwartz and Hendrick, two blond and blue-eyed Bostonians who liked the look of the Arkin girl and who made the deliveries to and from the café. As arranged with Felix Sommer, they removed money from the café's till for the salesman from Detroit to disperse to those who were players in the deal elsewhere. Ewan's mother was required by Felix Sommer to record the withdrawals from the till as expenditure on generator fuel or potatoes or some such thing depending on the amount collected by the boys. What Sylvie McCarthy got was to keep her job, since Felix Sommer was a man who appreciated acts of kindness. As Sylvie fiddled with the accounts book the two American boys liked to sit and drink coffee and smoke and watch the Arkin girl who had turned down their offers to be the meat in their Boston sandwich. When they came up behind her and clutched at her while Sylvie was out serving or in the pantry the Arkin girl turned on them with the meat knife and rolled it without fuss or frenzy in front of their throats, and they smiled like they knew what kind of game this was. When Felix Sommer came round, he told the Arkin girl, 'Just be civil to the boys. Is that so much to ask of someone who takes my wages every week?'

Under pressure from Felix Sommer, the Arkin girl finally agreed to accompany Schwartz to a dance being held by the Chamber of Commerce at the Civic Hall. Felix Sommer had the contract for the catering. Sylvie McCarthy said the Arkin girl was stupid to agree. Who was she to talk? the Arkin girl asked. Be careful, Sylvie told her. The girl shrugged and said sure, she'd be careful.

Before too long at the dance, the Arkin girl wandered off from the Bostonian and got to talking to Sol Werbernuik as if to be contrary, as if to suggest that she had done enough by coming to the dance with the Boston boy to meet her obligation to Felix Sommer. As if to say she could play by her own rules. As if to say there was an end to it. Naturally the Boston boy wasn't so happy.

The Arkin girl left with Sol Werbernuik half-way through the evening. They talked a little. Thinking it to be a magician's trick she asked Sol Werbernuik how it could be that he would be a writer. Sol Werbernuik told her how. He said that if you caught it right, words were like a glimpse into a writer's soul. He said if you wrote honestly enough about some small corner of things, all the truths of the world could be reflected in it. All that was needed was honesty and the bravery to set down words.

Some time after that the two of them were found on the lawyer's Georgian terrace close to the High Street by a small group of men that included the Boston pair and the salesman from Detroit. Which is how Sol Werbernuik came to be beaten up on the streets of St Agnes, though no one around at that time of the evening saw too much and was able to identify anyone involved in the beating. The local paper reported a brawl between American GIs, one of whom was treated in the infirmary before being ambulanced back up to camp.

The story of how Jonas Werbernuik broke into the pro ranks was as simple as it was beautiful. It had no more dramatic content than seeing a man stroll up to the front desk of a casino and cash in his night's chips.

Jonas, who had taken Edwin Haas's offer at the stadium where the Galleon City Mariners performed to work on the cleaning rota, did the long shift. Edwin Haas, General Manager of the Galleon City Mariners, had never heard of Pete Salinger, never come across the Furry Cat Pet Food Company, looked incredulously then laughed out of the side of his mouth around a half cigar when Jonas produced the tissued remains of the bogus contract.

Evenings were the most difficult to pass in the lodgings he had taken. It wasn't too nice a place, not like home seemed to have been, but it was dryish and folks left him alone if he kept the door tight shut against the noises of other apartments in the building that leaked through to him. Evenings were when people in Galleon went meeting other people, went out dancing to forget how things were, went to the pictures to see how they might have been, got drunk or high on benzedrine to feel how things ought to be. The man in the room above him saw spiders big as soup plates every night after *Naked City*. Evenings were a problem for Jonas. Jonas would have liked to go dancing maybe, but who'd go dancing in the big city with a stut-tut-tutering giraffe?

44   The Veil of the Temple

At work, around the stadium locker rooms and corridors when the office staff and the loose-limbed players had gone home for the evening, Jonas got to talking to Redford Washington, the man who did the rest of the cleaning. Redford Washington was a big-boned man with that easy enough approach to things which size and a certain weariness allowed. He was perhaps in his forties. Weight and suchlike made it difficult to tell and it was certainly the case that no one round about knew his age for sure.

Redford Washington was a divorced and private man, a sometime basketball player whose cartilage had let him down before it could see him through any kind of college scholarship. As a result, most of his life had that after-the-ballgame feel to it.

Some nights Redford Washington drank for supper, and some nights he played poker with Edwin Haas's friends who could, inevitably, mystically, clean him out at some three-quarter point in every game which meant the next night he'd have to drink to forget what he'd lost.

Redford Washington gave the appearance of having reached a truce, an accommodation with his aloneness in this world. The players and staff and folks in Galleon hanging round the Mariners kind of liked him but didn't know why and didn't feel too strongly about it. That would have pleased him had he known. Redford himself felt sorry for Jonas and the mean trick played on him by Pete Salinger the bogus scout. He felt like he and the boy were two of a kind though he in turn didn't quite know why and didn't feel too strongly about it. It just happened that he seemed to have an ear for the Werbernuik way of speech which cemented their alliance around the baseball stadium on its quiet days and its empty nights. Sometimes Redford Washington caught a clean sentence of the boy's first time, like taking a high, right-field ball on the run, without saying 'What?' or 'Shit!' or anything.

And so the weeks ran on. Jonas was happy to swab away in the hushed cradle of the stadium. Sometimes it was just so quiet in there he got to crying. He remembered the bit in the Bible where the veil of the temple had been torn in two and thought how much more daunting it would have been in silence than in a chowdering storm.

After work, he'd take a stack of balls from the stores and throw some pitches at the targets from the practice mound with just the one auxiliary light casting a dirty yellow on the stadium's darkness. Just Jonas and his broken dream and his simple love for the purity of the game down in the belly of the field on a Michigan night when everyone outside in the world who was home free from spiders and the like had gone dancing.

When he got back to his room Jonas washed down and watched old movies on the black-and-white TV, lying on the too-short bed and dozing through the flickering pictures on the screen, imagining he was maybe Spencer Tracy and that people loved and respected his countenance and voted for him or paid him money to open supermarkets or waved to him on their way to work. Ah me.

After the spider man who lived in the room up from Jonas and along from Redford Washington had quietened, Jonas generally slept like a log. In the mornings he walked through the park (having woken earlier than the hungover Redford Washington), fed the ducks far beneath him on the lake, and went to the stadium dressed in a silence he wore like a greatcoat.

Once or twice Jonas wrote to his mom, though nothing came back. By careful omission he tried to tell her he was doing fine without plain lie-telling and said he'd send a cheque through to her real soon to make up for the awful thing he'd done to her. After his work he'd practise once more, sending his box of balls one by one down through the gloom singing 'SSsss . . . wuoossh thuck, put put put' as the balls struck the pitching target and dropped, stung, to the earth. Except that one night from out of the darkness of the back seats as Jonas smote the target from the practice mound with his curve ball a voice said, 'Do that again, son.'

The voice, Jonas Werbernuik thought, was maybe that of Edwin Haas through the gristle of his evening cigar. The echo of his voice clinking down off the banks of bleacher seating

144

was like a fistful of chips being dropped on the counter of a casino ready to be cashed in.

45 'Going to the Champagne'

Until then, Ewan had barely noticed the Arkin girl. She was a pair of eyes watching him through the kitchen hatch. She was a curse or a slap when the Yanks misbehaved in the warm, narrow confines of the café. Everything else, looking back, had been filtered out. Boys would make fine navigators, Ewan thought later on in life. They focused on what was ahead of them and would not be distracted from their own line of vision. Which is why the sudden physical presence of the Arkin girl in his line of sight took him off balance.

Some days Sol Werbernuik didn't show at all. Some days Ewan found that Sol Werbernuik had already been in the café but had left on unaccountable errands before Ewan arrived. Sometimes Sol Werbernuik left notes for him which made the accident of timing seem less harsh. ('Jonas is pitching well – and two home runs for the Mariners that I hear the Babe would have been proud to strike.') Sometimes Sol Werbernuik left a book for him to read.

'Everybody was drunk,' Ewan read. 'The whole battery was drunk going along the road in the dark. We were going to the Champagne. The lieutenant kept riding his horse out into the fields and saying to him, "I'm drunk I tell you, mon vieux. Oh, I am so soused." We went along the road all night in the dark and the adjutant kept riding up alongside my kitchen and saying, "You must put it out. It is dangerous. It will be observed." We were fifty kilometers from the front but the adjutant worried about the fire in my kitchen.'

There were days when they met up and on those days Sol Werbernuik seemed as relieved as Ewan that they were back together, and Ewan's day would draw up life again. They would leave the café with Ewan's mother serving and the Arkin girl busy in the kitchen and they would walk along together through the town where the war's double summer-time held light in the sky till late in the evening with Ewan matching Sol Werbernuik's stride to fill the soldier's steps beside him. Sol Werbernuik would tell him about some crisis or development in camp, would ask Ewan how was his young friend, Lampeter. There was, Sol Werbernuik said, a copy of Walt Whitman's *Leaves of Grass* which maybe he would get around to letting Ewan read, but it was old now and not so well stitched along the binding and would need some careful looking after and had belonged to Jonas at one time who was greatly fond of Whitman. Back in the café, later, the Arkin girl would wink at them both as if Ewan knew secrets, and Ewan would ask when they would now play the World Series. The days ran by like a low fever.

Sol Werbernuik didn't seem to have changed. Perhaps he played with his spectacles a little more. Perhaps he laughed more and was more forgiving about his comrades. But all in all they appeared in Ewan's mind to have weathered the storm. There hadn't seemed to be betrayal in the air. There was, though, more vague talk of departures and of invasion plans for Europe and no date for the World Series and a generally untidy scrapping to make money and do deals whilst the Yanks were still around. Days ran and ran. Until Ewan, hurtling through the woods, spied the Arkin girl, skirt hitched above her blue-white thighs, straddled across the soldier's belly and the two of them scuffing and grunting and the soldier's pants slung over branches close by and Sol Werbernuik surrendering himself piece by piece to the Arkin girl who knew that he was her's now.

Three days after that came the order for the Americans to prepare to move out, but by then Sol Werbernuik had already disappeared.

46 Visiting the Sick

The firm of solicitors with which Ewan McCarthy served his articles after the war was over and its memory fading took part each year at Christmas, along with other companies, in a visiting scheme at the city's hospitals and homes. Companies supplied teams of usually junior employees to run visits to children in care or those who were sick. The climax of the scheme was a New Year's Eve party thrown by the Mayor for all the firms involved. The money raised from the tickets went to the Mayor's Charity but the real winners were the firms themselves who had supplied the scheme with bright-eyed young men and women taking time to help out, and the Mayor and all the customers for professional services in the city knew this and thought well of them.

Ewan McCarthy, eager and unsure of the road ahead, thought it only right to volunteer. Or rather he thought it wrong to refuse the invitation made to him by the firm. Young men were well thought of if they did and not if they didn't, and the scheme only ran a month a year for just an hour at a time, and that didn't seem so bad.

The first evening they sat Ewan with a girl who'd been injured in a boating accident in which the rest of her family had drowned. On the second, they put him in a room with a crash victim in a coma and suggested that he talk to her because a man's voice might some day help to bring her round.

'What should I talk about?' Ewan asked.

'Anything,' they said. 'It's just the sound of your voice.'

So Ewan told her, over and over, the story of Jonas Werbernuik and his gift and how he travelled hopefully on a bus to Galleon, Michigan, but however hard he tried the story never turned out well for Jonas.

One time he was outside a ward drinking tea which he'd managed to get from a passing trolley. Another of the young volunteers came by. She was a secretary with the same firm.

Ewan hadn't noticed her much before but here, in the hospital, throwing him a lifeline of smiles and conversations, she seemed a special kind of girl. Her name was Ann and she was transparently good at all this. Ewan it just made angry and defeated.

'What's the problem?' she asked, supping on his tea.

'I don't know,' he said. 'I don't know how to make them feel better. I feel like their chaos might drown me.'

The cheerful ones with half a body scared Ewan even more than the ones sucked of life – they had a stillness inside that evaded him – and some way through the scheme he packed it in, though Ann agreed to cover for him and do his stints. He thanked her by taking her to dinner in Manchester's Chinatown, where Ewan had been to rowdy meals when one or other of the articled clerks had a birthday and when each time, half drunk, he'd done his 'Americans closing in on Berlin' routine. Ann had never eaten Chinese before. She lived in a flat close to the city centre with two other girls and shared a landing and cooked with two pans on the stove top. She liked Ewan's smile, the serious way he went through the menu for her, his lack of trust as if he felt people were capable of knocking him from the high wire, his intensity when eating, the boy in him. And so they were married. They produced in due course three sons who, one by one, grew into adulthood and took up their own lives. And it was only after that, when she'd been introduced to some of trustees of the St Agnes Night Shelter at some function in the Civic Hall, that she came to take up work again herself. With the boys grown and only Tom still living at home, after twenty years of rearing Ewan's children and being a wife she suddenly had spaces in her days. One or two of the trustees spoke to her about herself whilst Ewan was across the room, and it was Jenny Aldred who teased from her the fact that she'd so much enjoyed the Christmas visiting scheme of the firm in Manchester they'd both been on when she and Ewan had met.

That same evening Jenny Aldred made her the offer to come and work as a volunteer at the Night Shelter. Ewan was reluctant when he found out. There was Tom to think of ('He's sixteen,' Ann explained). There was the nature of the clients the Shelter took in each night – this wasn't like playing doctors and nurses in the hospital – but Ann was adamant.

'It's something I want to do for me,' she said. And Ewan, spying a scene ahead, gave way and waited for reality to crease her bright notions of how the world really was.

By the time Ann had become a paid worker at the Shelter Tom had moved to London and was playing in a battered jazz club off Soho called the Paris Club run by a friend of his, living hand to mouth and with a girlfriend somewhere in the frame. (He wrote a postcard. It said, 'More bebop than Ellington soliloquies' and Ewan's heart sang.) Ewan in his fifties ran less and was balding and was on three committees and in the evenings walked his dog as far as Mahoney's Wood for exercise. Ann did some typing for the Shelter and worked through two nights each week. After her night on duty, she would arrive home in time to check the morning post and to make breakfast.

'How're the sick and the lame?' Ewan would ask.

'Still there,' she would say.

The Night Shelter was a target for local kids, the Denny Arkins and the like from the tenement flats, who regarded the

150

Night Shelter's clientele as fair game. Sometimes Ann bribed Denny and the others with Mars Bars or cigarettes not to smash the windows and pee through the letter box. Sometimes they laughed with her and wished her well and went home. Sometimes the next day the place would have been trashed again or spray-painted, or a drunk making his way there for the night assaulted or abused. Sometimes it was the Shelter's residents themselves who smashed the windows. Sometimes a doctor would have to be called out to section someone who'd gone berserk. Sometimes Ann would sit with some man through the night and he would tell her, clutching rosary beads or cigarettes, how he came to this and by talking he would find a chink of light in the way ahead and he would resolve to do something, but the next night or the next week or a year on he would be back, drunk or beaten up or in clothes he had worn for a month. And then the Night Shelter team, having found themselves back where they started, would begin again as if the past were not an obstacle and magic could still be worked.

'I can't understand it,' Ewan said. 'How can you keep believing that these people will get stronger and better than they are. How can you hide from yourself how things really are with them? Can't you see that they'll let you down? That there isn't always hope, or sense?'

'After you make the decision not to see,' Ann said, 'everything else falls into place.'

In the St Agnes of 1733 they queued for two days whilst the administration enabling men's souls to be saved in the typhus-ridden town was put in place. Sometimes men grew angry that their place in the line was being challenged unfairly and squabbles broke out. There was confusion early on about whether a man could queue only for himself or whether, with the right money about him, he could bring forward a dozen names to be saved. And more than one person asked if there were degrees of salvation and whether one man could be saved more than other, lesser men for a larger donation given to God. These things of course were crucial. There was a sense that time was scarce. If the Apostles had returned to their ministry on earth, who knows – maybe the end of things was near. Maybe the typhus had been a sign and, in that, St Agnes had been blessed and not cursed.

The blackamoor took down the details of each man as he sat at the table set out in the stable yard of the Wheatsheaf Hotel and stamped the certificate of salvation with a wax motif of the Church's insignia. Horace Weir himself blessed each saved soul by placing his hands on the head of the baptised man and by speaking as he did so in a mix of Latin and Aramaic which for all the local men knew could be a recipe for gin or a cure for old men's gout but which had a ring of authenticity about it.

It was only when one woman asked about her child that Horace Weir at last paused in his efforts. He grew sad. He was forced to concede reluctantly that these legal documents of salvation could not extend to minors under the age of sixteen. One couple whose two other children had died brought forward their one remaining boy of fifteen.

'Will you not let us pay extra,' they asked, 'for the boy's place to be reserved with us in Heaven for a little extra money in case the typhus should claim him too, or the world should only turn another week?'

Alas, Horace Weir said, children must continue to run the risk of hellfire and damnation until they reached the age of eighteen when their souls, too, could be bought positions at the right hand of the Lamb. That was when the fun started.

The bidding from one merchant to find a way to save the soul of his son went up to thirty-five pounds – three years income for some employed men. One man said that in return for saving his son he'd let old Horace sleep with his wife until the wife heard about it and stuffed her husband's head in the milk tub. But whatever incentives people offered him, Horace Weir was forced to go on repeating the injunction given to him by the Apostles in Jerusalem before he left for England – children not yet matured to eighteen in the eyes of God could not have places booked for them in Heaven. Some women wept that they had secured for themselves what they could not provide for their offspring. Only after several days of this, when almost all the adults of the town had subscribed to Horace Weir's church, when many a notable citizen had wined Horace and debated scripture and *summum bonum* with him to look for ways out, did the possibility of a solution to the conundrum appear.

One man, maybe a Summer or a Sumner – the records differ – finally struck a deal with the reluctant but persuaded Horace. In return for twenty guineas, the man's son of eleven was to be apprenticed to the Church of the Apostles as a supplicant and, sailing from Plymouth, travel back with Horace Weir's men to the monastery recently contructed on the Mount of Olives. There the boy would receive a schooling in the classics as well as scripture and be taught a trade with wood as Jesus was with which to go about the world. At sixteen he would spend three years as an adjutant of the Church and after that would be free to return to St Agnes with his passage paid for. Until the time of his return a stipend would be paid each year to the parents through the offices of the Bishop of Sutherland. More important than all of this, though, the boy's immediate salvation as a member of the Church, even though a minor under episcopal law, could be assured should the world any given day cease turning.

That night the man threw a celebration for Horace Weir and for his son's saving and for the ridding of the town of typhus (the quarantine, Horace Weir had persuaded the authorities, had just six weeks more to run), and before nightfall the following day the first twelve children had been apprenticed to the Church at twenty guineas each. They were made ready to leave before the week was out with the blackamoor and the two women who would escort them on the first part of their journey and pass them on to brother monks two-thirds of the way to Plymouth. They left St Agnes two days later having been given dispensation by the town's authorities (which by now was Horace Weir when all was said and done) to break the quarantine. The departing party was blessed before they went by the Vicar of St Agnes for a safe journey, and given the sacredness of their errand they seemed sure to be granted this.

48   Simple Sums

'Did you see Sol Werbernuik again after that?' Rachel Tallow asked.

'Not to talk to. Not at all really,' Ewan said. 'I caught sight of him I think as the Americans were being trucked down to the station on the day they moved out of camp. I don't know whether he saw me. I sometimes hope he didn't.'

'Why do you say that?'

Ewan shrugged and didn't answer her. 'What happened to him? I don't suppose he's still alive?'

'No,' she said, 'he isn't still alive. But it makes me happy to know that finally I've talked to someone else in the world who knew him.'

'I was his blood brother,' Ewan said smiling.

'I know,' she said.

'And you really are Sol Werbernuik's daughter?'

'I really am,' she said.

They stood above the town, leaning on the rails of the observation point. Below them lay the bowl of fields where in 1944 the Americans had based their camp and where once Sol Werbernuik had drawn a rectangle on the bark of a yew to mark the pitching area for the World Series game that Ewan and he were to have contested but which in the end never took place. After that was Mahoney's Wood, settled into summer now, and beneath that the houses of the town pitched between its six wooded hills, and the high road trailing off in the distance, going by the Seebohm Plant's two moons and scaffold architecture, and cutting the hills at the lowest point of their horizon.

'I didn't know anything about him until after David was born,' Rachel Tallow said. 'My Mum and Dad had never hinted about me not being their natural daughter. I guess it seemed like the right thing for them to do with the war over. You know – everyone starting life over, mending things and beginning afresh. They were living in Padiham at the time. There were lots of orphans. The war had seen to that. I suppose they just tried to shield me from things. Then Dad, Donald Tallow I mean, back from the war like everyone else, got a job at the Seebohm Plant and so we moved here. And until David was born, that was my life story – Dad got a job, we moved from Padiham, I grew up in St Agnes, then later on Helen came.

'I wasn't married when I had David. So there were the usual fussy whisperings about it. It made me worth talking about, for a while at least, which I suppose is how word got about. Then one day, not long after I'd had him, this woman came around. We thought she was selling something. But she stood on the doorstep – I could hear my dad talking to her – asking if she could have a few minutes to look at David because David was her grandson. I remember my dad threw her out and said she was a crackpot and told me not to worry, that she'd not be back again, that it was probably someone wanting to cause trouble because I wasn't married or else a crank from the infirmary. If she called again, I was to ring for the police. My Dad was insistent about that.'

'You never married?' Ewan asked.

'No.'

'What about the father?'

Rachel Tallow sighed and smiled. She seemed easier with the world when she was outside in the open, with space around her.

'It was a mistake. Me and him, I mean. Not David. David was a wonderful thing to happen, even if he was unplanned and unexpected. But Callum . . . He was a friend. He was nice, he was older than me. He wasn't the settling-down type. I think we were a bit drunk that night. We'd been out with a group of friends to a dance at the Civic Hall. We were good friends. We made each other laugh, but we'd have been lousy married to each other. We would have each ruined what the other was. I told him that. I told him I didn't want anything to do with him, no money – nothing, and that I'd bring the baby up and I'd love him and I wasn't going to make Callum marry me as some stupid insurance policy for my baby's welfare. And that way I'd be able to think fondly of him and not hate him which would have happened if we'd tried to stay together.'

'How old were you?'

'Nineteen. I'd had plans to be a nurse. I wanted to travel. I'd been to Morocco the previous summer with two friends. We went to the Isle of Man. We used to go to Blackpool for weekends in the summer and stay at a guest house run by a little old lady my mum knew.

'He was twenty-eight or nine or something. He got on with his life, I got on with mine. He left town later on. I've never seen him since. I'm glad because I still like him. My life was David after that. It wasn't a tragedy or anything. It was just something that happened. And I did what I said I would. I brought him up and I loved him and he made my life . . . whole, I suppose.'

'And Sol Werbernuik?'

'Ah, Sol Werbernuik.' She turned away to face the woods and the town falling away below them.

'A week or so after my Dad had turfed the woman away from the house, she came back. My Mum and Dad were both at work. She came during the day, knowing, I suppose, that there'd be just me and the baby in. She would have been forty then, and her name was no longer Arkin. My Dad would say that to look at she was rough at the edges – though she'd obviously been a good-looking girl in her time. I was a bit lonely at that point. Tired and getting used to the strain. So I let her in and brewed up and we sat on the settee drinking tea, with David lying between us half awake after his bottle. She was very quiet about things. Wary I think. She said at the outset that she didn't want anything from us. She said she wasn't coming to lay claim to David or me or anything. It was too late for that and besides, she said, she had nothing much to offer.

'Afterwards, we'd see each other every so often. We'd talk a little in passing and she'd hold David's hand, but she never fought to make it more than that and I never called her Mum. I still see her round town now and then. We pass the time of day. It's not easy knowing what to say all the time.

'In a way she was more bothered about just seeing David the once than in seeing me or getting to know me. She sat on the settee with his hand on her palm. Seeing him gave her a line back to Sol Werbernuik that she wanted. It was all she dared ask for.

'She started talking about herself after that, and she showed me a couple of photographs she had of Sol, and that's how I found out about him that afternoon – that I was his natural daughter, that this lumpy woman sat next to me on the settee touching David's hand was my real mother, and that David was Sol Werbernuik's grandson.

'Checking everything out was, I suppose, just a case of doing some simple sums, although I think I knew she was telling the truth as soon as I saw the two snapshots of Sol Werbernuik. And then later, as if to prove it, David grew up into the image of the man in American uniform in the black-and-white photograph. He was shortsighted and he even wore the same kind of wire-rimmed glasses. They made him look bookish, though he wasn't really. She gave me the photograph to keep that afternoon. When I turned it over it had "SW, St Agnes 1944" scribbled on the back as though she feared she might one day reach some furthest point from which she would be unable to remember or to find her way back.'

Rachel Tallow had been born to the Arkin girl in the early days of 1945. Sol Werbernuik hadn't replied to her letters about the child she was expecting, or the birth when it came. She had continued writing to him at the battalion's pre-invasion base in Devon for several months after the Normandy landings in the hope that these letters and cards and pleas for him to write would be passed on. But finally, she gave up trying to contact him and put the child up for adoption at Easter through the Catholic nuns in Padiham.

At the orphanage she sat the child on her knee and together they looked through the windows at the Padiham streets outside.

'Promise to be good,' she said, and pushed a silver shilling into the girl's tiny hand and turned and left the room. The infant Rachel lived in the care of the nuns at the orphanage for eighteen months until she was adopted as a toddler by a couple called Tallow who believed at the time that they couldn't have children, although Helen's arrival six years later disproved the diagnosis they had been given.

The Arkin girl married Solomon Heaney in 1947. They had no children. Solomon Heaney, who at twenty seemed to be one of the boys and spirited and full of cheek sufficient to draw her out into the present, spent a lifetime on the fringes of poor deals and small defeats in St Agnes, easily led by his younger brothers who were faster and smarter than him, and feuding with the Arkin clan around the tenement flats and in the town on Saturday nights with beer inside them. Ah, how she'd come to believe she might escape from all of that.

By the time she came calling on Rachel Tallow for that one afternoon twenty years later, she was sometimes being hit by Solomon and had put on weight and sometimes cried in the street and had to assure people that there was nothing wrong. A few years later she was discovered by hikers on the moors after she'd been left for dead. It turned out to have been Solomon who'd done it with four days wages in Scotch inside him. He spent three years in Preston Prison, but when he came out she let him home again after he promised he'd mend his ways. Some promise, Mitch Murray might have said. Some promise.

'What happened to Sol Werbernuik?' Ewan asked. 'Why didn't he write back if he thought he might have a child?'

'He didn't suspect,' Rachel Tallow said. 'He didn't know.'

She told him that six days before the Americans moved out of St Agnes and decamped for Devon Sol Werbernuik had been put on a charge, accused of pilfering stock from the mess stores and selling it to middlemen in town through the Last Chance Café on the Padiham road. It was revenge, Ewan only now realised, on the part of Stolley, the salesman from Detroit who hadn't been able to coax Sol Werbernuik into joining the scam. After three weeks under confinement, during which the company had moved south through England from Lancashire to Devon, the charges had been dropped and he had rejoined his unit in time for its final preparations for the invasion. The letters, Rachel Tallow was sure, never got through to him. There was so much chaos in those last weeks leading to the landings in June. In Devon the Yanks had commandeered three thousand acres of land to practise the invasion. There were a million and a half American soldiers in England by then. He never got the letters, she said, and Ewan knew that she was right.

'He died in Normandy,' she said. 'Six days up from one of the beaches the Americans landed on.'

'She told you this?'

'No, no. She didn't know. I think it was more than she could face to go looking. No, it was me who found out. A while after she'd been to see me I got in touch with the American Embassy in London. They were very helpful when I said Sol was my father. They had someone search it out for me and found out that Sol had been killed in the first week of the invasion. He is buried in the American cemetery near Bayeux. David and I went over when he was eighteen. I have the letter from them. They even sent me a family address in America but I never used it. I couldn't see the point, and I didn't want to go upsetting my mum and dad. You can have it if it's any use, if you still want to take David's case up for me.'

50 Some Men's Particular Smile

Ewan read through David Tallow's diary twice more, first to set the details in his own mind, and then to draw his own working notes from it – dates and names; readings. He also asked Rachel Tallow for photographs of her son. She went through her albums with him and he settled on half a dozen which he then had copied. They showed David as a boy, as a young man, at different stages of his illness and one a week or so before he died. These he pinned up on the cork notice board above the work desk in the study he used at home.

He began to delegate some cases to juniors, to Harris Leary the Fifth and others, cases which he might normally have taken himself. He asked the other partners if they'd take on more through the summer since he wanted to take some time off and wanted to work more on one particular case. He wouldn't say what was preoccupying him. Trust me, he said, I think it could be important in the long run. I want some time to run with it and then I'll come clean. Really, he said, I think it will be worth it in the long run for all of us.

Sure Ewan, sure, they said. Some thought it might be connected to the landfill deal he was helping to negotiate for the site of the soon-to-close zoo. Maybe he was sorting himself a slice of the pie. Maybe he was the middleman. Maybe the firm of Murray Associates would be a winner in all this as well. Maybe he'd got into woman trouble, some said. It didn't matter. Ewan was a safe pair of hands. He'd be all right. He'd get back on track when it mattered. It was a while before it started to leak out that Ewan was preparing a case against the Seebohm Plant.

The photographs of David Tallow were slowly surrounded on the noticeboard in Ewan's study with notes and observations, sometimes a question or the name of a man or a number of men out of town he had to go and see. He felt it better to keep things to himself and away from the office until he had a full tale to tell. The notes grew like leaves on a tree and the face of David Tallow, looking so like Sol Werbernuik in those rounded spectacles and with that smile and serious air, looked out at him as Ewan worked.

'He had this look about him,' Rachel Tallow had said. 'Sometimes I'd say "What are you thinking?" and he'd come back to me with a start and look at me for a second like a stranger. Then he'd smile. Some men's particular smile comes from a deeper place than laughter or amusement or being one of the boys. That was David. Such a smile he had – like children smile when they're alone and content with the world. I think he kept a part of his childhood intact in him when he was grown. I think even the illness didn't destroy that in him.

'He thought being an engineer romantic. He used to say that unravelling secrets and finding answers in the world was a little like falling in love. He always said he never had the time to be married. A group of them used to go climbing in the Lakes at weekends. Until he couldn't any more. Until he was too sick and he couldn't go.'

'He knew what he wanted to do pretty much from the off, I think. That's why he felt so betrayed in the end. He started at the Plant at seventeen, and later they sent him to college to get a degree and then come back to them. He did a sandwich course over four years whilst he was still working at the Plant, and he was on the student board as well. He used to joke that he was the only one who never had time to sit down and eat lunch while he was there. He used to joke a lot. Even towards the end he joked. I remember him being so much more alive than other men.

'It's funny about children, isn't it? There's so many times when you can't help but worry because their grip on life seems so tenuous. One missed breath or a gust of wind or a passing bus might crush them, and there would be an end to it. I used to fear for him coming down the stairs, or swimming, or climbing steps on the playground when his legs were too small to make the stride, but he was so independent and wouldn't hold my hand. Always throwing himself into things as if he felt himself to be immortal or protected by God. And so you let go fearfully and pray that all will be well. Then later you see them in a new life, a different way, and they seem so remarkable and indestructible and fiery and you can only marvel at the thought that you were a part of their fragile and haphazard creation. Do you know what I mean? And you start to hope yourself for their immortality.'

Ewan knew what she meant.

She talked about David a lot like that to him. It seemed to help. What she said, the timbre in her voice when she spoke of her own son, made Ewan think of Tom. Of the way, when Tom was still living at home, he had played bebop tunes on his piano in the dining room when he had been up, and Duke Ellington soliloquies when a day had beaten him and the only comfort had been in letting his sadness seep out in the music. One time, years and years ago (Tom couldn't even have started school then) Ewan had taken him to have three abcessed teeth extracted – Tom who was resilient and angry at any kind of restraint and four years old. Ewan could still remember the sweat of them both from the fear of the thing when Tom came round, shocked and whimpering, clinging to him and appalled to be bleeding at the gums. The scent of gas was still sweet on his boy's breath, the smell of blood warm in his mouth close to Ewan. Ewan could remember the bursts of crying and dozing and more bleak crying through the long afternoon and into the night as Tom clung to him, afraid to let go, lacking faith in the world. Ewan could remember thinking he'd rather have his own tongue cut out than put the boy through the outrage again. But by the next morning Tom's faith in things was back and he was bowling through his clattering days again.

'One of the doctors at the Salford hospital towards the end asked me, if I were given the choice by God, would I swap places with Tom so that he could live? I said that, given a choice, I'd trade David's plight with anyone else in the world if it saved him for me. Isn't that a terrible thing to admit? I suppose that was a mother's answer again.' She lowered her head to find some privacy for the thought away from Ewan.

'Do you believe in fate?' Ewan asked her. 'That things happen for a reason?'

'No', she said. 'I believe in opportunities. I believe some-times there are choices.' She bit her fingernail. The wind blew around them on the hill.

In the weeks that followed, Ewan McCarthy, statesman of the town, seeing life now in St Agnes uncovered and afresh, had

so much energy about him that he felt himself reborn. He felt
he had the strength of ten men. He felt himself to be captain
in a harbour readying to take on nets and square things with
the harbourmaster and set sail for Cape Breton and, before a
week or two was out, return with his catch safely on board for
the astonished and rewarded people of the town. And even
after seeing Gabriel Snow and hearing the man's doubts and
confusion, Ewan knew that now was the time marked out for
him to win over the people of St Agnes and make David
Tallow's death worthwhile and in doing so restore to life the
legacy of his own blood brother of half a century ago – Sol
Werbernuik. It would take a man of Ewan's stature, but
finally he had come to see what all those years of building up
a solid reputation were for, like saving shillings in a bank
patiently, year after year. In his fifty-eighth year Ewan
McCarthy had found a way to round off all the awkward
edges of his life and make a whole, and all would be well. All
would be well.

51   Seeing Gabriel

Gabriel Snow wasn't so big, or so doomed, as Ewan had
believed. He lived out near Euxton and seemed happy enough
in a restricted kind of way. He was neatly bearded and thickset
and wore a dull green shirt and brown corduroys. His flat was
at the end of a row of six, one flight up and bordering the
goods yard of the railway station. He had that awkwardness

that made him good with women and strangers. He had impatience, which he didn't mind showing by saying what he saw. He had a kind of Cornish melancholy which Ewan felt he had tried to hide. Ewan liked him and was wary of him.

'If you sit down,' Gabriel Snow said, 'at least there'll be room enough for one of us to cough.'

The kitchen was the size of a cupboard and allowed Gabriel Snow two steps in to make the tea and room to turn to bring it out again.

'You live on your own here?' Ewan asked.

'It's good to find a lawyer with a sense of humour,' Gabriel Snow said, and smiled his own particular smile. 'We have met before though,' he said. Ewan couldn't remember.

'Your firm helped me to buy my house when we moved to St Agnes. When I came up from the West Country in the sixties to work at the Seebohm Plant, when we came here to the promised land, you did the conveyancing on the house.'

'Did I? I have to say I can't really remember. I thought I only knew you from the newspaper reporting. How was the house?'

'Smashing. Bit of damp in the kitchen. Bugger next door with two lorries parked outside and a dog that barked till midnight. But as houses go, not bad. We were happy enough there for a long while. Until the shit began to hit the fan as you might say.'

'I'm glad the house was alright,' Ewan said. 'I'm just sorry it all ended like this for you.'

'Are you? I can't say I am. Well, Jean was a bit miffed I suppose – losing the house and everything – which did kind of finish us off as it happened, but I'm really OK with things as they turned out. You think of me as deprived because I catch a bus and don't have two acres of garden and dog muck to mow?' He grinned, which left Ewan feeling wayward and not sure how to proceed.

Gabriel Snow's flat was worn and not so comfortable. The walls of the living room were lined, though, with books – books stuffed this way and that, wedged vertically and horizontally onto orange-crate and raw-pine shelves, books ring-bound and with broken spines and with car boot sale prices tatooed on them and with coffee rings and without thought or order to their cataloguing. A tiny television was crammed into a corner, dwarfed by an armchair worn at the sleeves and by a plucked rug which spread its way half across the room.

Ewan wandered round the books while Gabriel Snow finished making the tea. His library seemed filled with crime writers and clever thrillers. Strange reading for a bigot, for a crude, short-tempered Cornishman with a persecution complex. There were some gardening books, some social history. Books to kill time and deaden days, he could imagine Sol Werbernuik saying, pushing at the glasses on his thin, New Jersey nose. He mentioned this when Gabriel Snow stepped back inside the room with the tea.

'Well there you go,' Gabriel Snow said. 'It's that lawyer's streak in you, got me cornered already.' He seemed unworried by it.

'I found a Hemingway somewhere,' Ewan said.

'You like Hemingway?' Gabriel Snow asked. 'I have most of them somewhere.'

'Yes,' Ewan said, 'I like Hemingway. And you?'

'He's a shit,' Gabriel Snow said matter of factly.

'Hemingway?'

'A shit. Made his life up as he went along to fit his fiction. Not a privilege granted to most of us, you would agree? Got hit with bits of one stray shell while he ferried chocolate bars, never fought with the Italians, or with anybody else come to that, like he led people to believe, lived on the backs of the French and his wife's trust fund, hobnobbing till he hit it big.'

'How come you keep the books?'

'He writes well. Though of the Americans I prefer Steinbeck. A decent man. A good reporter of the state of men's souls.'

'You're not an easy man to please.'

'Oh I don't know,' Gabriel Snow said. 'I always thought my tastes were simple enough.'

'But not for the Seebohm Plant. Or for its masters.'

'Well no, no. But then there really was no pleasing them. Not when I kept asking them what they thought were the wrong questions, and they kept giving me the wrong answers, and reminding me of my social obligations. They thought as a manager I should be more responsible, especially since I'd signed the Act.'

'The Act?'

'Official Secrets. Using that stuff's a mucky business, you see. I was just far enough up the slippery pole to have to sign my soul away.'

'Is it true,' Ewan asked him, 'that once you threw paint over the cars of people sent by the Plant to barter with you about the Augee case?'

170

'Yes, it's true. But then the bastards had just burgled me the night before. More fool them for leaving the paint.'

'You knew it was them?'

'You know many burglars would take documents and leave cash?' Gabriel Snow said. 'Anyhow, that's how they found out I'd removed files from the Plant. The ones they wouldn't release anyway because they said they'd been destroyed in a fire in the Admin Block. That's how they got enough to sack me and discredit me, and since I didn't have the files any more I couldn't hit back.'

'You're not involved in politics any more?'

'I never was involved in politics. Just in men's lives. People forget that when it started it was just one manager taking up the case of one man, Ben Augee, dying of a radiation over-dose.'

'But no more?'

'Not in campaigning, no. Not since Ethel Augee's death. That kind of finished me off. I liked her. I wish I could have done more for her.'

'That was a sad accident.'

'Well yes,' Gabriel Snow said, 'that a woman could mistake a sofa for a reservoir.'

'You don't subscribe to the coroner's view that it was an accident? You think she killed herself?'

'Well like I say, a sofa can sure look like a reservoir in a dim enough light. That way no one needed to suffer the shame or inconvenience of it. I guess her light must have been pretty dim at that point. She was missing for four days before the body was found. It was swelled like a zeppelin when it floated to the surface. Like gas trapped in a pigskin. Sometimes there's no dignity even after death. What the hell. Whatever, I know that I wasn't a good enough man to persuade her that justice was round the corner.'

Gabriel Snow described himself now as non-aligned. Maybe he'd just run out of steam, Ewan felt, in his fight against the Plant. Maybe he'd lost heart, or belief that he could keep going. People, Gabriel Snow said, nice people, people who had a greater good to defend, told him that truths were lies for so long that it started to corrode away his own life. And so now he raised plants and read books and had a new life growing. He helped to run a seedling nursery supplying garden centres and the like, public parks. The Seebohm Zoo and places like that, though the zoo's orders had tailed off in the last year or two. He said he liked the simplicity of it. Things grow and die, he said, and I am a conjurer with it.

He knew David Tallow. David had worked for Gabriel Snow when the boy had first gone to work at the Seebohm Plant as an eighteen-year-old. It was he who had gotten David Tallow on a degree course. Long after they had kicked Gabriel Snow out for gross misconduct, David would stop him in the street and talk to him as if Gabriel were still a human being. There weren't so many did that for him once the men in grey suits had started working their own brand of magic on him and on St Agnetians and turned Gabriel Snow into Satan, and local men with wives and church habits peed through his letter box and sent vomit to him in the post and ate his liver as though he were Prometheus each day for years.

What Gabriel Snow liked most about his days now was the quiet. He didn't have waterfalls and fears like earthquakes in his head. He grew seedlings from nothing and read books and even had friends again whom he played darts with in a pub on Thursdays and he slept at night. He hadn't, though, changed his mind about things. When he went, he said, he would go with a clean conscience and a poor list of achievements which he accepted was a compromise but was better than nothing. And then he asked Ewan a question.

Did Ewan know, Gabriel Snow asked, that David Tallow was the fourteenth person working at the Plant since 1952 to die of causes attributable to radiation discharge? And did he know about the cluster of childhood leukaemias in St Agnes, starting with Helen Tallow and finishing, if that was the right word, with a four-year-old who as they spoke was hairless in a Salford clinic? A cluster which was higher than the national average, higher than those around Sellafield or Springfield or Dounreay? The figures for St Agnes would have shown it, but the figures were altered. Not out of wickedness. Out of faith that things could be put right and were best done so quietly. 'And then the files I'd got hold of had to be got back. For the sake of the people. For the sake of St Agnes. A little town like St Agnes, Mr McCarthy, is a lifeboat in a hard storm some way off shore. What you can't afford, so the theory goes, is one man rocking the boat or everyone will start to fear that they will drown. That's what the bastards rely on.

'A bit of harm for a lot of good. There's this unspoken trade-off behind all of it because they don't know the truth of it, how safe or unsafe it is. They gamble and sometimes the lying is part of that. Behind the statistics and the smiles, they gamble. Half a dozen lives, a dozen, fifteen like they had at Vorderrhein, a hundred, a thousand, in this generation or the next – in return for energy to help us live and to save us from darkness. Christ, it's so reasonable. Don't you think? Its so fucking reasonable a deal.'

52 Giving Judgement

It became the custom for Horace Weir in that typhus ridden summer of 1727 in St Agnes to adjudicate on disputes between citizens. Seven months of typhus and the resulting isolation of St Agnes from the world had led to a number of difficulties between people. Men who couldn't move their animals to market owed rent. Men who practised trades which depended on an influx of people passing through, men running inns or shoeing horses, borrowed money and built debts and reneged on payment dates. Families lost breadwinners. Men died and were buried on top of other men in communal pits. Others rowed and bickered and some fought, and some said Hell was here till Horace Weir arrived and built order on the chaos and saved men's souls at five shillings a time and proved it by virtue of certificates.

In the mornings Horace Weir administered the scheme which took on children into the Church of Apostolic Truth to send them half a dozen a week into apprenticeship at the church's monasteries abroad which was how come they were allowed out beyond the sentried boundary markers. In the afternoons Horace ate, sometimes dining with citizens keen to honour and feed him – he had a severe appetite for food – and then slept. In the evenings he held court on the raised plinth in the Wheatsheaf and men gathered round whilst Horace Weir, a freeman of the town by now since investiture by the Vicar of St Agnes, heard cases brought by one man against another in the absence of a circuit judge.

Some nights Horace Weir prophesied for them. Like the time he said the sky would be lit up by shooting stars from heaven at midnight the following night to show God's pleasure in the path St Agnes was taking. The next night well men stayed up and watched the sky and saw at midnight a shooting star rise above a whiff of gunpowder from the Padiham hills and across the black night and more than ever things seemed closer to the end of the world than folk dared to say out loud. And people whose children had gone – been apprenticed abroad to Horace Weir's church – breathed easier that these children were saved if Armageddon came this week or next.

After that Horace seemed to gain some confidence and began to take more of a hand in the running of the town. He changed the tax regulations so that rich men in the town paid one third of all their wealth into a kitty which was shared out amongst all the poorer ones. Merchants and the like were made to do menial work, to serve in the sickhouses or carry out the dead to the burial pit, and how the mass of people laughed at that. Some clever fellows, lawyers probably, asked him what right he had to issue edicts like this when all he was

was a travelling preacher but Horace Weir reprimanded them and told them to give unto Caesar what was Caesar's and to give to God what was God's. Horace made blacksmiths into magistrates and farm labourers into officers of the peace. Horace ruled that hats or stockings could not be worn since God and the returned Apostles preferred that men went about clean-headed and unadorned. The gentry complained that all respect and social order had broken down, but those who complained too much about these things had their houses confiscated by the new magistrates and handed to the people and the people laughed the more about it when fine gentlemen went knocking on the poorhouse door.

Maybe because the end of things seemed close (through the prevalence of death, and lights in the sky, and men without livelihoods, and typhus fleeing town dressed as a bear), Horace Weir's decisions handed down at the Wheatsheaf sometimes seemed strange, unusual. No doubting, though, there was logic to them, and wisdom.

When two men claimed ownership of a milking goat and neither would yield (there was a dispute over payment involved) Horace adjudicated that the goat be cut in two and each man given half. Oh, the blood and screeching there was that day before each man was given his portion of the animal. People agreed, though, it taught everyone a lesson.

One woman alleged the attempted poisoning of her and her husband by her husband's family who had feuded with them for years. After that, since no one knew how widespread the plot ran, all meats and wine, fruit and cake and preserves had to be conveyed to Horace Weir's suite at the Wheatsheaf for him to taste and confiscate where there was any doubt or concern.

Then Horace agreed to sleep with two sisters after their father (who before Horace's arrival had been the magistrate) accused another man of deflowering them, and the verdict was that they weren't virgins after all and that the father, who was saying at this point that old Horace was a fraud, should be flogged for being mischievous and reckless with his charge and so he was in the courtyard of the Wheatsheaf with Horace and the town looking on for sport.

The mass of men who were still behind him began to ask Horace whether he couldn't stop on when the quarantine was over, at which point they would make him Mayor for all that he had done. Horace Weir turned them down, although he showed no signs of upping sticks and moving on as yet. Two men who claimed that Horace's church was a fake and objected to his nonsense were found guilty of wearing hats and dandyism and had their property and assets confiscated and distributed to the poor and were made to serve at table when the town gathered at the Wheatsheaf Hotel each night. Yes, Horace Weir seemed quite settled in the life until one night when he was holding court at the Wheatsheaf and twelve children sent to join the Church's order in Jerusalem turned back up in town filthy and exhausted and saying they had been sold for adoption to people in Suffolk and Gloucester and some in Ireland who had already been sent by boat to Meath and Wicklow. These twelve had run away at Birmingham after they'd heard the blackamoor conclude the deal, as he'd done with the others, on Horace Weir's behalf and taken payment for them.

The typhus ran another seven months. Horace Weir some-how escaped from custody, issuing his promise in the process that one day the bear would return and seal the fate of the rest of St Agnes's children. The blackamoor and the two women, though, were hanged. Twenty-eight children of the town were never traced. No record was kept of those in St Agnes who, with the benefit of their certificates of salvation, made it to Heaven in the end, or those who did not.

53   Gifts for the Voyage

Rachel Tallow asked Ewan how he had found Gabriel Snow.

'I found him different,' Ewan said, 'from what I'd ex-pected.'

Gabriel Snow had given him the notes he had made based on the files from the Seebohm Plant which had later been stolen from the flat. Stuff he would have used if the Augee case had ever come to court or to an inquiry. The original files, Gabriel Snow said, showed the Seebohm Plant and its masters cheating with the figures, suppressing others, distort-ing still others. These were amongst the ones lost in an office fire following an accidental release of emissions inside the compound in 1987. Gabriel Snow also gave Ewan one of the cuttings he had on his kitchen ledge. It was little more than a stick in a yoghurt pot. When it was full-grown and a lilac bush, he said, Ewan would be a wiser man than now. Ewan took it graciously as the gift of a well-meaning but punch-drunk boxer. Finally, fetched down from his raw-pine shelves, dusted and long since creased, he gave to Ewan a battered copy of Hemingway's *First Forty-Nine Stories*, this volume published in 1944. Gabriel Snow had smiled when he had given it to Ewan. A good year that, Gabriel Snow had said, and Ewan had agreed.

Ewan said to Rachel Tallow, 'Your father left home at fifteen. His parents had died and his uncle brought him up running a bakery in New Jersey.'

'You know all that?'

'He showed me what he wrote sometimes. He went to work on whaling boats off Newfoundland. Learned how to build the wooden ships they still build there. He spent time in Maine fishing for lobster. He did something in Nebraska and lodged over a whorehouse. He wrote stories. He was going to get them published after the war.'

Rachel Tallow pulled the photograph of Sol Werbernuik from the purse in her shoulder bag. 'My father, Sol Werbernuik. A writer.' She shook her head, smiling and awed to believe this, holding out the photograph for both of them to see.

'Till now, David and I loved him without knowing anything about him. Just his face and what we could imagine in him.'

'One time,' Ewan said, 'the mizen-mast broke when they were two days from shore, and two men died in the struggle to make for home.'

'It makes me brave,' she said, 'knowing that. When I see him in this photograph, always thirty-four years old and in a strange country and before he died and with hope and possibility in his eyes that he will use everything that he has seen and felt and be a writer one day, it makes me think that everything is possible.'

That night Ewan spoke to Ann. He told her that with Rachel Tallow's blessing he would use the leverage of what little evidence he had to re-establish the local consultation panel which, through the District Council, channelled local views to the Seebohm Plant. He said that he would ask that the Plant's sale to the private consortium based in Berne who ran the Vorderrhein plant be suspended and an inquiry set in place in light of this and of the safety record at Vorderrhein. And in St Agnes he would convene a public meeting in the Civic Hall. Ewan would use the meeting to set out his fear that the fourteen deaths since 1957 when the new power station had been brought onstream might have been disguised or covered up. That children's deaths in St Agnes could be linked to the Plant. He would say that David Tallow's leukaemia could possibly be traced to a 1987 release inside the plant. He would not, he said, set the public meeting up as a means of lobbying for support or for the gratitude people might feel (although this would be fine) but because of the need for it – to persuade the people of St Agnes that all of this was necessary, best in the long run, to persuade them to trust him, feeling sure that St Agnes would be grateful finally for the truth. In this way Ewan would, after all these years, loose the moorings which had held him fast and safe, slipping slowly out to sea, and wonder how things would be on his return.

54   Rocking the Boat

It has rained for two days and the boat is open to the sky. Sometimes people stop as they drive past on the back road to watch Ewan McCarthy building his ark which can be seen of course from down in the town, to watch him labour in the rain around the three-quarter-built Newfoundland whaling boat, windscreen wipers whipping back and forth, then drive on.

The rain sings into the wires, making the ship hum. Ewan McCarthy, winter mud to his knees, forces wooden planks into place on the half-done deck cabin and Salazar hammers them home. Salazar, whose hands burned when they set the guy wire up, has raw red lines across his palms but just grinned at Ewan after the wire smoked across his flesh.

The swells of rain have hit the side of the boat and the covered hatch all day. Beads stand on the grey gloss where they have painted 'Good Hope' on the rising bow. Heavy clouds have chopped and swum in the sky from early morning. The wind which brings the rain sprays the grass around them. Once, Salazar slipped on the wet boards of the deck and Ewan grabbed for him and held him, and they steadied themselves on the rail of the deck even though the blunt nose of the boat stayed rock still and only the rain rolled around them and ran down off the scuppers.

Back in the shelter of St Agnes, below its six hills, there have been two sightings of a bear reported to the press. Horace Weir's bear, perhaps. The papers have run the two stories straighter than they did when Salazar went to them about it. The bear, the paper said, was seen each time in the woods above the town. If only we could find the bear and shoot it, men said, maybe the consortium would agree to resume the purchase of the Seebohm Plant. Maybe Ewan McCarthy would retract his foolishness then. Maybe our livelihoods would be secure again. But Ewan by now was away from the harbour and saw no bears.

55 Taking Leave

The order to move came suddenly. The city of tents on the fields above St Agnes began to dissolve in the storm and scurry of men. The news came down that the Americans were leaving. By dinner time they would be gone, and Ewan waited for Sol Werbernuik.

People lingered close to the High Street knowing that the convoy must pass through on the way to the railway station. Some, women mostly, ran to the station and fought for their places there because there would be no other way to take their leave of men they had come to know all of these slipped-past months. Already, though, the MPs had sealed off the station and there was no way through and nothing to be done but to wait. Women held each other. Women who had loved Americans, or who had fancied that they had, or who had loved the adventure and the abundance of it all. Women who had come alive in the secrecy of what they had come to know.

Women sad and curious and amused and moved to be here and to wait.

Ewan McCarthy, on the hill outside the camp, was worried about where Sol Werbernuik was. They had plans to make. Ewan was to safekeep Sol Werbernuik's stories, the ones with him in and the others. They had the rendezvous to plan for when the war was done. But still there was no sign of him.

The Americans, victorious and on parade as the trucks passed through the streets, grinned at the carnival of their departure. They threw cigarette packets to faces they recognised as truck after truck went by towards the station. Other men, bent forward in the trucks away from the back flaps, sat morose and still and wondering what would happen next. They were like the men they had been before the war in their own small towns and big cities – some caught up in the moment of the thing and others melancholy and reflecting upon it.

Ewan McCarthy stood on the pitcher's mound, in the field behind the camp. As each squad of men came by, fetching or carrying beyond the wire, he looked into their faces but in none of these groups did he see Sol Werbernuik. He kicked dust from the mound and waited. When he couldn't wait any longer he went round to the main gates. There were other boys there too. As the last trucks rolled out of camp, and the city of tents came down leaving nothing but fields of grey and yellowing grass and worn earth, Ewan stood by the road shouting Sol Werbernuik's name into each truck, shouting and shouting again, but they could not hear him for the noise. Ewan felt the strain of shouting lumping up in his chest and the sting of the dust thrown up by the lorries in his eyes. It began to be possible to believe that Sol Werbernuik, was in each of the passing trucks and that each time Ewan shouted his name he didn't reply even though he had heard him. Each time there was a truck there was another chance that Sol Werberbuik was in it, but each truck came and went. Down in St Agnes someone was ringing the church bell, but Ewan just cried and shouted at the last of the trucks and in the end there was just a ghost camp and a few MPs and the last details of soldiers mopping up what there had been of the camp, and Ewan, defeated and absurd and drowned by engine noise, shouting 'Fuck you, Sol Werbernuik, fuck you' to the last trucks rumbling by down the hill and somewhere a bell knolling and MPs smirking at the boy and soldiers smoking in the clattering trucks on their way down to the town.

56 The Return of Pete Salinger

In the days after his first match for the Galleon City Mariners, a double header against Duluth, Jonas cut out the reports which appeared in the *Galleon Sentinel* and in the *Chicago Tribune* and in the sports magazines which had taken reports on the wires. There were some optimistic assessments that the Mariners had maybe found a pitcher who could throw them out of their early season slump and, as games went by, some of the East Coast papers took up the story in a small way.

Jonas sent the pile of cuttings in a shoebox to his mom who never did see them, having died in Schaeffer's store not too long before. It wouldn't be until the season's close that the shoebox reappeared for him through the mail marked 'Return to Sender'.

In the letters that he sent alongside the cuttings (which all eventually came back to him) Jonas added a cheque now and then and asked for forgiveness and suggested that his mom come out to Galleon sometime and watch him play for the Mariners. He wrote to her in his letters that he had finally made it, that he'd become what he was meant to become and now folk would respect him for filling his allotted place in the world. For playing ball. He didn't though, in any letter, mention to her about Pete Salinger turning up.

Half a dozen games into his late starting season with the Galleon City Mariners there was a rat-a-tat on the door. Two days more and Jonas would have moved on. Edwin Haas had found him a cleaner place in a half-decent brownstone where no-one saw spiders and anyone drinking did it out of sight behind closed doors and not on the front steps or on the fire escape. Two days more – but then timing had always been the hallmark of Pete Salinger's game.

'Aren't you gonna invite me in?' Pete Salinger asked.

Jonas, not knowing how to say no and not knowing what to say, said yes, and Pete Salinger came in and after a little while sold Jonas his pitch.

Pete Salinger explained to Jonas how things had happened. How Pete was an agent not for the Mariners but for several other teams all of whom had their quota of rookies already for the season, which is why Pete sent Jonas here to Galleon – knowing, just knowing that Jonas would make it. He couldn't bear the thought back there in Scared Heart that Jonas

185

might not get a stage on which to make use of the gift of his talent.

'Jeez,' said Jonas, 'I never suspected all that,' but Pete Salinger was already away, looking in the refrigerator for food.

Pete Salinger hoped that Jonas would forgive the ruse with the fake contract, but how else could he have got Jonas out here under the expert eye of the Mariners' coach, of er . . .

'Edwin Haas,' Jonas managed to say clean out first time.

'Edwin Haas, exactly,' Pete Salinger said. The expert eye of Edwin Haas who was bound to take Jonas on once Pete had gotten Jonas 'the Giraffe' within spitting distance of Galleon. Having seen the reports in some papers, Pete Salinger knew this to be true. And as if to complete the whole deal Pete Salinger had set in motion that long time ago in Scared Heart he said here, here's the forty-eight dollars we said we'd reimburse once you made it here safely, and he handed Jonas the money.

'Now,' Pete Salinger said, 'you'll need an agent since you've hit it big. People will be hitting on you now. There might be contracts. The major leagues could come in for you at the end of the season. It's just as I saw everything stacking up but you'll need an agent.'

The result was that when Jonas moved apartments two days later he moved with a flatmate, with Pete Salinger who was now also his agent. They sorted out a bank account – Pete Salinger did – which they could both draw from. Pete said he'd been to see Jonas's mom (she was well, Pete said and wished Jonas well and sent her love and things), and Pete Salinger would set up a trust fund she could rely on with some of Jonas's money.

Pete Salinger introduced Jonas to some other people. They were his friends, he said, and now they were Jonas's friends too and they came round often to the apartment. Jonas was grateful, although he didn't often stay up late playing cards with them since his sore and too-tall back needed resting after a game or a day's practice.

57   Betting on the Outcome

Jonas kept on pitching well as the Mariners moved into mid-season, even though his back ached mornings and after games. Pete Salinger's friends, who were now advisers and the like to Jonas, had him seen by a specialist who promised to send through the report in time. Jonas's friends in turn sent him to a chiropracter who whistled in awe at the shape of the boy, laid him on a slab and bent and stretched him for a week and his back grew easier. In the game against Evanston Jonas, uncurling the arch of his back, shut out their batters for three straight innings and Galleon won by five to one to move within two games of Oak Park, who headed the table. In the triple-header in Madison, against the Chiefs, Jonas all but wrapped up the whitewash on his own. Some major league scouts were reported to be seen taking notes at the back of the bleachers out beyond right field and everyone knew they were there to watch Jonas 'the Giraffe'.

With two games to go in the regular season and the Mariners bidding for the league pennant if they could turn over

Oak Park in the double-header came the bombshell delivered to Jonas by Pete Salinger. It was Jonas's back, Pete Salinger said. The specialist's submission seemed to spell an end to Jonas's career. It said his back would be lucky to hold out the season. Pete Salinger sympathised with Jonas about his back. He sympathised, too, about the fact that Edwin Haas would likely as not dump the Giraffe at the end of the season rather than risk a new contract. Pete Salinger knew Haas and knew he was a bum and wouldn't ever stand by a man in need. Don't worry, Pete Salinger said, though. His friends felt it appropriate that Jonas deserved a testimonial for his services during this one brief season of pitching glory before he'd have to return to obscurity. The guys had clubbed together their savings and their winnings and come up with an astonishing eight thousand dollars which they would be pleased for Jonas soon to accept as his testimonial. And all Jonas had to do this one last time before his back finally gave out was to pitch badly against Oak Park so that the investments made by these same men in favour of Oak Park triumphing over the Mariners at nine to two for the pennant would give a good enough return to help them realise their wish to provide poor Jonas with the testimonial he deserved.

Jonas was reluctant, but Pete Salinger spelled out for him how Edwin Haas would never risk any kind of new contract, with the likelihood that Jonas would have to quit before too long with that oh-so-sore back he uncoiled each time he pitched. Pete Salinger brought out the testimonial contract for Jonas to sign. It offered him the eight thousand dollars to be cut from the winnings from the money staked on Oak Park taking the division pennant.

In the first game against Oak Park Jonas pitched badly and the 'Os won six to two. The 'Os best hitter, with a look of Scared Heart's Tommy Schaeffer, struck three home runs off balls Jonas had all but tossed across to him. He lolloped round the bases grinning from ear to ear. Passing Jonas, he looked up and winked at him each time.

It seemed strange to Jonas to have catcalls tumbling down to the field from the stands. Christ's sake, kid, Edwin Haas said, what kind of pitching was that? Do you want a contract for next season or what?

That night, feeling lower than he had ever done when he had been cleaning up around the stadium as Redford Washington's apprentice, Jonas determined that he couldn't go through with his agreement with Pete Salinger to throw the fixture, eight thousand dollars or no eight thousand dollars. The next morning he hunted out Pete Salinger to tell him. Pete Salinger's face grew still and thoughtful. You do what's good for you, kid, he said, speaking quietly and as close up to Jonas's face as Jonas's six foot ten and some stature would allow. You're a smart kid, with a lot of good fellas backing you who want a little something back in return. Don't you go letting down your friend Pete and his associates after all they've done for you.

Jonas hunted out Redford Washington to ask him what he should do, but discovered that Redford Washington had gone to ground having run up debts in a new card school run by friends of Pete Salinger.

As the team warmed up for the second and final game that night, some people in the stands booed Jonas for his display in the previous game. Jonas started off pitching badly again and in the first three innings the 'Os struck two homers and were well in control of the game. The Mariners were subdued, thrown by the sudden decline of their star pitcher. Someone in the dugout had an evening newspaper which two or three men were passing round amongst themselves. The paper reported that Redford Washington had been found beaten and shot dead in downtown Galleon, seemingly after some dispute over gambling debts. Jonas read the piece then went to speak to Edwin Haas who was watching the Mariners fail to make anything of their fourth innings. Jonas asked the coach about his back. In his fury Jonas's stammer had all but gone. Edwin Haas said he didn't know what the Christ Jonas was talking about, the team doctors had given him a clean bill of health at his signing-on medical, and Jonas had better buckle to in what was left of this game or he'd need a medical when Haas had finished with him.

Jonas pitched for the next two innings like he'd never pitched before. In shutting out the Oak Park batters, people said they couldn't remember seeing anyone pitch that quick before or with such a peculiar, angry torque. In the stands Pete Salinger sat watching with a still expression on his face. At the bottom of the eighth, with two out and the bases loaded, Jonas unleashed a pitch to send back the 'O's Tommy Schaeffer which Schaeffer, shaping for a grand slam, never saw and which knocked over the backstop. The backstop threw off his glove and men gathered round to inspect his blistering raw red palm. When they looked back to the mound in admiration, Jonas was bent over and holding his back and struggling to straighten up. His team mates got him back to the dugout, but he had to be carried to the dressing room and a doctor called.

The doctor suspected it was the effort of that one last remarkable pitch – the effect of that peculiar whiplash action Jonas had summoned up. Whatever he'd put into that single pitch, it seemed it was unlikely that Jonas would ever pitch again. It wasn't, though, until the following day's paper caught the scoop (the one that showed how Jonas had thrown a game on behalf of a group of gambling men who'd bet on the Oak Park 'Os winning the pennant) that men stopped feeling bad for him.

58   The End of the Season

In all the years that followed, Ewan McCarthy could never have the story finish any other way than this. Ewan didn't know how Sol Werbernuik had intended the tale to conclude but, no matter how and when the notion of Jonas Werbernuik arose, once the Americans had gone Ewan could never find it in him to picture Jonas making good with the Mariners, or for Pete Salinger to be caught out, or for Jonas to triumph beyond the closing season over the guile of a hard-bitten world. Always the story ended that same way and maybe that was right. Who's to say?

Whatever the reason, it seemed that the incident at Lampeter's house just after the Americans left truly marked the end of the season of possibilities and that after that Jonas would never see things through.

A few days after the Americans had pulled out of St Agnes, Ewan went round to Lampeter's house. He knocked. Mrs Sommer answered. Ewan asked if Lampeter was in. Mrs Sommer watched him as though she had not understood. Ewan thought she had not heard him. Then she turned and went back inside the house, leaving the door ajar and Ewan waiting. A few moments later Felix Sommer appeared at the door. Ewan asked again. Felix Sommer said that Lampeter had died. He said that Lampeter had died of the illness he had had all this time. He said Lampeter had been dying all these years. He had no wish to make it easier for the boy.

The season was over. The days grew leaner. People didn't talk so animatedly in bars and in the streets. The bleachers stayed empty. People battened down for a different season. No, no matter how Ewan tried, poor Jonas wound up beaten by the ingenuity and art of other men and having missed his chance. It was Jacob Seebohm finally who saw something of this in him and took him under his wing.

'When I was a boy of four or five,' Jacob Seebohm said, 'I had the notion fixed quite securely in my head that I would pass this way again. That everyone would pass through things again as though sequences of events were corridors that stayed to welcome us back again the next time and the next. As Orthodox Jews, this notion and how it came to settle on me must have puzzled my parents and outraged the Rabbi. I would say to my mother or my father, "When I am here again and a boy again I shall choose to go that other way." I do not know where it came from. The world about me I suppose. It created a sense to things that ritual and prayer gave to my father and his like. My father was upset by this, but his brother, my uncle, persuaded him to leave me be and not to chastise me for it. My uncle was a wise man, don't you think? He saw it for what it was, a passing fancy to make sense of the majesty and perverseness of life opening out around me. And lo! – now I believe in other things.'

Each day after school as Ewan edged into manhood he did his chores at Seebohm's zoo before meeting his mother at the café and heading home with her for supper. The animals, which Jacob Seebohm chose to believe were the souls of former men, stood steadfastly whilst Ewan swept up their excrement and the straw it lay in and whilst he filled their troughs or threw them meat or leaves or whatever sustained them in the lives before they became men again.

When the zoo closed at dusk and the few people still in the zoo heard the bell and left and the wolves howled in celebration and the animals, excepting the single, spectacled bear, became themselves in their natural lives again, Jacob Seebohm would appear and spend the evening walking the grounds and inspecting the animals. Sometimes Ewan would walk with him and heard Jacob Seebohm enquiring of each animal how the day had been, and absolving each one of sin and giving it a name, referring to a macaque, say, as Joseph DeLoach or to the spectacled bear as Thomas Grierson. Once, he spoke to a capybara as his grandmother. He gave them all histories. He made them carpenters and bankers and factorymen in their former lives as men and guessed at what they'd be next time, 'although I don't know for sure', he reassured Ewan. 'It's just an instinct – a guess, you might say.' He gave them every job that sprang to mind – except for that of lawyer since his uncle had been a lawyer and the profession seemed to be exempted from this scheme of things.

Jacob Seebohm's uncle had fallen in love with a distant cousin during a gathering at the family home in Saxe-Coburg and they had married and settled eventually close to her people in Kiev and his uncle had been killed in a pogrom in the town in 1892 when all Jews had been beaten and their shops broken and businesses rifled and some torched.

'Some men cannot wait to surrender their brains for the instincts of pack animals or of bears,' Jacob Seebohm said, and he maintained a reverence for the job of lawyer for as long as the young Ewan McCarthy knew him. He nodded approvingly when Ewan himself said he thought he might become a lawyer.

'Are you mad because of what happened to you?,' Ewan asked. Ewan knew by now of the months of detention, of Seebohm's breakdown, and of how Seebohm had come to found the zoo.

'Do you mean crazy or angry?' Jacob Seebohm said.

'I don't know.'

'Me neither,' Jacob Seebohm said, 'but see – I can smile and I have the souls of men all around me to care for and I can hope that if I come back as a goat or a capybara some crazy old man will offer me in turn some small piece of affection.'

Jacob Seebohm told Ewan that he'd make a fine lawyer. Not immediately, since growing up (the process of discovering that what goes on in the world is different from what goes on in men's heads) and learning what men are takes time. But eventually he would be a fine lawyer and learn how to use words well.

Jacob Seebohm explained to Ewan that the Hasidic commentary on Noah told how when God ordered Noah to build the ark he used the word 'teva'. In Hebrew, teva meant both 'ark' and 'word'. In the final reckoning it was by building words that people would survive the Flood. Though he conceded that words, carefully reckoned, and a respect for other men had done his father's brother little good in the long run.

In return, Ewan told Jacob Seebohm that a few days after the Americans had gone, on the day Ewan had found out that

Lampeter had died and had been dying all the war, a parcel
had arrived at the café. It was an unthreading and tattered
Leaves of Grass. Walt Whitman. It carried no inscription. It
was from the American Ewan had known.

'Words, you see,' Jacob Seebohm said. 'Always words.'

60   Say It Isn't So

It is incumbent on a blood brother, no matter whether a gap
of fifty years or more runs on and whether a man is in the
meantime lost or changed or presumed to be dead, to track his
brother down. It is true that the memory of Sol Werbernuik
faded at first. It seemed to grow less relevant for a time, for a
few years, half a life, through Ewan's entry into the world of
good fellows and his training in law and his rising in the firm
of Murray Associates back in St Agnes and his being honoured
by people for his dextrous skill with words and cases and his
ability not to get entangled by life and its living. It grew faint
whilst he found a wife whom he loved for some time and then
at least was comfortable around; whilst he had children who
filled his days with this and that. But through all of this the
spark lit by Sol Werbernuik was never entirely put out so that,
as Ewan grew up, his memory and belief in Sol Werbernuik
grew a little brighter and more relevant and wistful, and
sometimes he worried that too much had been given away
and once or twice a year he'd worry about what was left and
he'd drink coffee or a Scotch and listen to sad, jazz tunes and

think about a big house in the distance and hear that windy night outside which he imagined to be buffeting brave travellers. So that in the end, as men came to see him, worried about Ewan's stated aim to rally support for an inquiry into the Plant's safety record and into the death of David Tallow, and said to him that he'd only bring harm to things by doing this and said in so many words, 'All this aside, boy, what do you believe?,' he might well have said, 'I believe that once there was an American called Sol Werbernuik who built trawlers in Maine boatyards and sailed Newfoundland whaling boats and whom I loved.'

Ewan wrote to the New Jersey address which Rachel Tallow had given him. The reply took three months. It came a week after the first brick came through his window. The reply was from a woman called Silva who ran a beautician's on the premises and sub-let the upstairs rooms to a Christian Scientist healer. Mrs Silva had held the lease for six years. Before that there had been a hardware store. She understood from people round about that at one time the shop had been a bakery, though she had no knowledge of a Jonas Werbernuik or of his nephew and she suggested City Hall Records. Alternatively, Ewan could try contacting a Mr Levin, who came once a week to see the man upstairs concerning his tumour, and who'd lived all his life two blocks away and did remember some things, although they didn't all tie in with Ewan's story, and it was better if the two of them corresponded directly. She gave an address. Ewan set his story out again and sent it off to old Levin, wondering what Mrs Lalas had meant by what she said.

Sol Werbernuik had never killed a man and never gone to jail, never robbed a bank or poisoned anyone. He worked in the bakery in the basement with his father, and his mother served out front through the day. They were Presbyterians and shy people, first-generation Americans, and they believed that God intervened on behalf of good people everywhere and doubly in America.

Sol Werbernuik never had an uncle. Sol himself slept during the morning. In the afternoons he went to the public library. He read books through the evening and worked with his father baking bread through the night and into the dawn ready for the new day when the same would happen again.

When Sol Werbernuik was seventeen his father found to his astonishment one day that he had an ulcerous stomach. It got worse, as these things do. They prayed. After a while he couldn't do the work any more on any regular basis so Sol did more and more, and his father just complained about the quality of the bread and stamped about upstairs, and Sol's mother waited each morning for Sol to finish baking, so that over breakfast she'd have someone to talk to before Sol slept. And Sol Werbernuik read and read in his room over the shop and in the public library and never built trawlers in Maine boatyards and never sailed Newfoundland whaling boats or sung the 'Marseillaise' over any quiet town one night, except in his heart. He lived all his life over the Werbernuik Bakery in New Jersey and did what had to be done and wrote stories although none of them were accepted by the magazines. He never married and he never saw a man die and he never did this and he never did that because his life was carved before he'd even lived it. That is the special curse of most men. Then he was called up because the war was on and, although he could have put it off because of those dependent on him, he went. The night Ewan got the letter from old Levin saying this, or as much of it as needed saying, he said a prayer for Sol and called him blood brother and loved him all the more for seeing him in that cramped and laboured life and how in that small space he'd breathed enough to keep his soul alive.

Two months later, Mrs Silva wrote to Ewan again. The Christian Scientist healer upstairs had been having a clear-out and had found a shoebox in the attic with letters and things inside. He'd shown them to her and Mrs Silva recognised them in the aftermath of Ewan's contact with her as Sol Werbernuik's things. She would be happy to send them on if Ewan wanted them.

There were some stories Sol had written, some from before he'd joined the army as a thirty-three-year-old rookie, some from his time in boot camp in Saratoga, some from England which he'd mailed back for safe keeping. The letters from the Arkin girl sent to him in Devon were there, together with a journal he had kept in England which he'd sent back in bits and bobs and which his mother had filed in the box ready for his return. The last section of his journal and the Devon letters had been forwarded by the Army after his death, along with other personal possessions. There was a baseball mitt.

'Jonas Werbernuik was six foot ten but he knew himself to be small under the stars,' Ewan read, his left hand in the mitt.

'What are you reading?' Ann asked. Ewan showed her. That night he confessed to her about the Augee thing.

61 Going Home

She was simply standing there, Ewan said – Mrs Augee. Not moving. Thinking but not moving. It must have been seven years ago, or eight. Sometimes it was not so easy to remember. There were so many people to be helped, to be Ewan McCarthy for. She had no coat on, which was odd, but people were grown-ups, even swampmen were grown-ups and could stand with no coat on out on cold nights just thinking things through if they wished on the banking of the reservoir up past Mahoney's Wood whilst other men walked their dogs.

Ewan stood watching her. Hemingway, still young then, two or three years old, stopped trying to edge away on the lead and sat down and waited for Ewan to resume. Ewan stood and watched her. The rain had stopped and the leaves and the grass had that gentle pop and hiss about them which follows rain on slow nights and the ground smelled sweet and Ewan found it amusing to watch her before heading for home. What seemed so odd was that she didn't move. She only stood there.

It was dark and getting darker. There was some light on the surface of the water but Ewan couldn't make out any expression on her face. It occurred to him to shout or walk over to her. But what would he gain by it? She had sometimes been his client, although for the case against the Seebohm Plant she had taken Gabriel Snow's advice to get an out-of-towner, not that it had done much good. It wasn't like she could tell Ewan anything out here he didn't know or which would help more with anything. She'd want to talk about things over and over. She'd say weepily, 'I should have gone with you, Mr McCarthy.' She wouldn't let go. People like that never let go.

Once, twice, again, he did think of moving toward her but his inertness echoed hers and he was powerless to intervene. Her stillness and his were part of the same single pattern of things. Finally the dog shifted its weight and moved him on along the path. Five steps, ten steps, then a noise that could have been anything, could have been the wind on the water, anything. Ewan turned round. She was not there. She had been standing on the bank above the water but now she was not there. Ewan turned and walked on, encouraging the dog to follow. Come on, boy, she's gone home. Sensible girl has gone home. Just you see, she's gone home.

But she hadn't gone home.

People used praise at first, and flattery. You've been around a long time, they said, and Ewan agreed. He'd been around a long time. What worried Loesser and the grinning Harris Leary (these days carrying that paunch of his like a baby) was the damage all this might do to the prospect of the completed sale of the Plant to the men from Berne who ran the Vorderrhein Project and who had feelers out about Lagos and the plant in San Sebastian as alternatives if a hitch cropped up here. What worried Loesser and Harris Leary were the second thoughts such men might have about investing in the Seebohm Plant, in St Agnes, if the Plant were to be dragged into the spotlight (and Vorderrhein with it) at such a time as this. Go back to Rachel Tallow, they pleaded. Persuade her one more time. See how much she'd want for a settlement and for some move away from here so that the rest of us can press on with life. She would get crushed in court, Loesser said sorrowfully. It was clear to him she couldn't be thinking clearly as things stood. You can see where her best interests lie, Ewan. Use that charm of yours to get her back on track and safeguard the future of the town.

Men stopped him in the streets or said about him that he was playing with their lives, playing God.

'You haven't seen the evidence yet,' Ewan told them, knowing he could swing this thing as he'd swung others.

'We needn't see the evidence,' they said. 'We mustn't.'

But still Ewan had faith.

'Men can pick holes in anything,' people said, 'if they search and pick for long and hard enough. Everything's a poison if taken to excess. Sometimes a happy compromise is best and more people are left happy than not that way and St Agnes will still be in in some people's top ten now and then. Our children will have a future, which is surely as much as they deserve, and who are you to deny them that?'

His colleagues at Murray Associates were sympathetic too.

They knew how easy it was to get ravelled in the plaintiff's view of things and have your judgement knocked cockeyed or impaired by pity or by sentiment without the prevailing experience of colleagues to balance things.

'Your career's too good to jeopardise on this,' men said who'd voted for him as Townsman of the Year not so long ago. 'Think of those people you haven't yet helped if you go down this road and things go awry – the Salazars and the Denny Arkins of this world who need you, ship-anchor that you are. What of your family, Ewan? Your wife. Think of your poor wife.'

And what of Salazar?

Ah, Salazar, who once knew Hell as some men do and came back but with only half a tale to tell.

The bear finally showed itself out in the open. It was a huge creature but no bigger than Salazar had imagined it. It pitched itself in battle against the big man and Salazar fought it all through the night. The man upstairs heard the crashing and the yelps and saw things on the grass beneath them the next day where they'd landed after being thrown through the open window by Salazar or by the bear. It went on till after two in the morning and someone called the police. Eventually Jenny Aldred was brought in since there was a suggestion that Salazar be sectioned, but Jenny Aldred and Salazar finished the night sat on the floor laughing about the bear and it seemed that the fight had been some kind of turning point and that after that lay only a long journey home from another country.

When Ewan came to ask him to help him build the ark,

Salazar told Ewan that he'd finally come to see the bear as misunderstood and said they had reached an armistice. As the ark took shape Salazar even had a notion to stow the bear away on it when the boat was complete to keep the animal safe since by then it was being hunted by men from the town with rifles who ran patrols around the woods hoping to shoot it and thus to lift Horace Weir's curse on them and save the Plant, and Ewan said, 'Sure, big man, sure.'

62   Waiting for Charlie Parker

Ewan picked Tom up from the station.

'How are you, son?'

'I'm fine. I'm alright.'

'How's Chrissie?'

'She's fine too. I'm sorry about Hemingway.'

'I know'. Ewan said. 'Have you heard anything from your brothers?'

'I got a card from Hugh on my birthday. Lawrence forgot. It'll come a month late. It sometimes does.'

Ewan watched him whilst he grew accustomed to the house again. It was a year since Tom had been back last. He had something to tell them, he'd said in the letter. Chrissie had gone to see her folks in Somerset.

They sat on wicker chairs on the patio above the garden and drank tea from big mugs whilst they waited for Ann to come back from the Shelter.

'It's funny how things turn out,' Tom said.

'Sometimes it is.'

'We somehow didn't expect Chrissie to get pregnant.'

'It wasn't in the plan?'

'No, it wasn't in the plan.'

'Are you pleased?'

'Yes I'm pleased. I'm really pleased for Chrissie, she's chuffed to bits. I never thought of me as a dad before. I mean, you never picture Duke or Satchmo changing nappies.'

'Will you stay in the flat?'

'We'll have to really. It's not ideal. It's only one bedroom.'

'What about the club? Are you still playing there?'

'I'm still playing.'

'That's good.'

'That's what I came to tell you, Dad. The Paris Club's closing. Ray can't take the losses any more.'

'How long have you known?'

'Three months.'

'What will you do?'

'I've been doing some part-time repping for some people Ray knows. It's helped to make ends meet when there hasn't been the money to pay me for a week or so. I even got myself a suit. Me! In a suit! You'd never have believed it, would you?'

'No, I wouldn't.'

'There's an opening to go full-time with them. So I've taken it.'

'What about your playing?'

'I guess that's the end of my jazz life. Maybe I can take it up again when Charlie's twenty and gone to college.'

'Who's Charlie?'

'Charlie Parker. What else do you call a first-born son? Anyway, who needs music night and day.'

'Playing jazz was all you ever wanted to do. You're good.'

'I know I'm good. Lots of people are good. There's more people playing good jazz piano than people prepared to pay for it.'

'There's no chance of finding somewhere? Someone who's heard you play?'

'Oh, if I was on my own, or even if it was just me and Chrissie, I'd give it a go, risk it, and if we got hungry one week I'd busk a bit or try to pick up some session stuff or even cook pizzas in Ray's pizza parlour. But with the baby on the way . . . you just can't think like that any more.'

'You'll like the repping?'

'No, I don't think so. But it pays more than the no money Ray can pay me. And it's like they say, I'll always have Paris.'

Ewan smiled at the bad joke. The two of them, waiting for Ann to come back, looked out at the garden where once Hemingway had dug and snuffled, and Ewan told the story of Rachel Tallow and Sol Werbernuik for his son.

63 Queensberry Rules

Loesser at least had the good grace to come and tell him what would happen.

'What do you think, everybody's going to play Queensberry Rules?' he said. 'Where have you been all these years?

And by the way I'm not here and we're not having this conversation.'

'I just wanted to know what the truth was,' Ewan said. 'That's all I still want. I want to know if the Plant was responsible for David Tallow's death like I think it was, and maybe for some others.'

'Why, for God's sake? It's gone. Safety systems get better every year. We keep learning. And we all know there isn't enough evidence to convict in court. That's why you're going for an inquiry. Why bring all this up now? Jeez, you pick your time, don't you?'

'How can campaigning for an inquiry and holding off the sale whilst it's done be damaging? It'll help in the long run. People will be grateful in the long run.'

'You think?'

'If I get the people on my side at the public meeting then there'll have to be an inquiry.'

'People will hate you in the long run. Don't think this is Queensberry Rules. Say, is it true that you once shopped Harris Leary for fiddling with your wife?'

Ewan showed Rachel Tallow the journal and the stories Mrs Lalas had sent him from America.

'They're yours, you should have them,' he said.

'I'll do you a deal,' she said. 'I'll take the journal and have that to read. Maybe I'll even give it to my mother. I'll think about it. And you keep the stories. I think they are more for you anyway. What do you think?'

Ewan agreed. He did not tell her about the Arkin girl's

letters reaching Sol Werbernuik in Devon. It would have been wrong to tell her. It would have been too much like judging him, and who knows whether he had planned to write to her once the war was over and stories of his had been published. Or whether he feared being found out for his small and necessary lies. Who knows. Sometimes such things can't be known for sure. Sometimes second guessing is the bigger sin.

64   Pieces from Sol Werbernuik's Journal

June 6.   I have sixty rounds of ammunition. I have one set of 'K' rations, a medical pack with morphine and tourniquet bandage. Amphibious gas mask. We embark from the ship onto the landing craft. There are thirty of us in the boat. The boat circles the ship whilst the assault wave is organised. The swell is rough. The spray blows into the boat and everyone is soaking wet. Some of the men in the boat are sick. Short of the shore the coxswain says he cannot get us any closer to the beach.

As the ramp lowers, the German machine guns begin firing. The first man off is first hit. The next man down is Schwartz, one of the two from Boston and he is also hit. Stolley, who has bribed his way to the back of the boat, sits there saying under his breath, 'It's murder. It's just murder.' I pray, 'God, give me guts'.

As I come out, I trip and hit the water all askew. For a minute the sound of gunfire goes blank on me. As I surface, it returns and is all around me. I see Indian Joe in the water. I am scared to hell but I want to survive.

When I get to the shore I look back. The sea is turning red. Men around me cry – I hear them. Schwartz is crying. The noise all around is awesome. Stolley has soiled his pants. How many of the men were got before they made the shore I can't tell. I know that Stolley and Schwartz have made it ashore but I don't think anyone else from our boat does, and our Company is so shorn of men that no one seems to know how to proceed or what to do next now we have made it to the beach.

June 8. Four a.m. A mile inland. Everyone sleeps in slit trenches, but real sleep is impossible. We do two hours on guard, two hours looking for sleep. It is a long night. My rifle is propped between my knees. The sky is black with bombers. Fetching and carrying death strategically.

June 9. We are set the task of taking Carentan. As we make progress through the fields today we pass cows dead with their four feet bolt upright in the air. Along the canal and down the lanes we move two by two. We pray that the other man will be our guardian angel. Sometimes men are picked off by sniper fire; those of us who aren't are sick with fear that we may be.

Schwartz and Stolley are both injured. They are treated by the medics when we regroup in the corner of a field, Stolley screaming, Schwartz still and grave and his face clenched as they stitch him as best they can. They are taken back to the rear field hospital somewhere near the beach.

And me? I have one thought running in my head. It is that I have to make it through all this and remember it and write it down if I am finally to amount to anything. It's not bravery. It can't be that since I'm scared as hell. But it gives me something to hang on to. Some men are white with fear. The eyes of some blaze out, like the world just went mad. But me, I'm just remembering so damned hard. In all my life I wanted to be a someone. Maybe this journal will be my chance. Maybe this – to come to hell and watch the sea turn red and see men who were stronger than me wet their pants – is the only way. So I watch and watch like hell which stops me from getting too scared. In a kind of prayer, I see the boy in Lancashire. I wonder if this is madness. I see Nick Adams and he tells me not to be afraid. He says he knew about me all along but it makes no difference to him. He says one day we'll sail for Cape Breton together. I say, 'Sure kid, sure.' And I wish him a good life.

Carentan. June 12. Word is we have taken the town. Maybe the worst is over now.

There goes Ewan McCarthy, the monkey strangler, people said. Out to get revenge on the Seebohm Plant because Harris Leary fiddled with his wife.

Within a month people had the measure of Ewan McCarthy. They knew about him ratting anonymously on Harris Leary and screwing up a talented man's career. They knew about the macaque. They heard Ewan McCarthy had a record of annoying women and making unwanted approaches to them – witness Jenny Aldred, a social worker, who tried bravely to stress when she was interviewed that nothing sexual had happened between them and that her comments to a colleague once some years ago had perhaps been taken out of context. It was known that he had once screamed abuse at some loonies in the social services centre, which seemed symptomatic of a life gone wrong. He had hit someone.

Then someone dug deeper and came up with the war. There had been an investigation shortly after the Yanks had gone into the embezzlement of US army property in St Agnes. The trail had led back to the Last Chance Café on the Padiham Road, where Alderman Felix Sommer, away attending at the deathbed of his only son, had been taken for a ride by people using his café to traffick in all kinds of goods. No charges had been laid but the trail ran all the way to Ewan McCarthy's mother and to the Arkin girl and a GI called Werbernuik who'd fucked one and maybe both of them, and maybe they were in the whole thing together. Sylvie

McCarthy had previously run up bad debts and had seen the ownership of the café taken from her before Felix Sommer had set her up to run the place, and was it any wonder that Ewan had learned to be so devious and to bear so much ill-will coming from a background like that? How far a life can fall from the dizzy heights we are prepared to grant it, people said. How small and shabby a life can sometimes seem when it is hauled into the light and held up for inspection. How easily are trusting people taken in. How necessary that we found out just in time.

It seemed an easier thing to do to resign from the firm. No one was too surprised. It was fairer on the firm, Ewan said. He didn't want Murray Associates muddied by the affair. Some Harris Leary or other with a boy's moustache and a habit of calling everybody 'mate' took it over and delegated to his heart's content and quietly found fault with most things Ewan had done and wondered if Ewan should maybe have gone a little earlier, but enjoyed the view out of the window up to Mahoney's Wood and insisted on shaking Ewan by the hand whenever he caught sight of him in town and wishing him 'bloody good luck'.

It was harder for a man to go walking without a dog. It seemed more suspicious, more premeditated. Mahoney's Wood had been partially cleared and built on. A residential nursing home eighteen months old was sited at one end. It was pleasant enough and landscaped and some of the trees had been left. It was an improvement on the industrial units which now stood where once old Seebohm's zoo had been. The rest of the woodland had been bought for houses. They would be three-and four-bedroomed and each built with cosmetic differences to please the wives of the purchasers. They were not intended for the Salazars and the Denny Arkins of this world but for professional men.

The fields beyond the wood where the Americans had once camped were still intact and you could still see from the vantage it offered down into the town three quarters of a mile away. Most days after tea Ewan walked there.

'I'm not so sure if I went wrong or whether I simply misjudged things,' Ewan said.

'It's difficult to say,' Sol Werbernuik said.

'I thought I knew folk better.'

'Sometimes that's the case.'

'Once I knew a man called Jacob Seebohm. He was the same.'

'That the guy that ran the zoo?'

'That's him. I think old Seebohm misjudged things. And Mitch Murray did in a different kind of way.'

'Maybe all you can do at the end of the day is chisel out your own perspective. Everyone sees things differently after all. What's up? Are you telling me you had a wasted life or what?'

'No,' Ewan said, 'I don't think so.'

'There you go, Nick Adams. So, How's the Tallow thing doing, anyway?'

'Not so good.'

'What you gonna do?'

'I don't know. Carry on, I suppose. I get tired sometimes. No one hears me.'

'I hear you. Ann hears you. Tom. Salazar hears you.'

'I mean down there. I feel like Noah saying that the Flood

will come and people look at me and see blue skies and cirrus cloud off in the distance.'

'Maybe you should build a boat. For when the flood does come.'

Ewan smiled. 'Jacob Seebohm told me this thing,' Ewan said to Sol Werbernuik. 'He said when God told Noah to build the ark he used the word 'teva'. And in Hebrew teva means 'ark' but it also means 'word'. People would be saved in the end by building words for each other.'

'You said no one would listen to you about the Plant.'

'You see a crowd here?' Ewan asked.

'But if you build an ark, a whaling boat like I used to sail, if you build it up here where everyone in the town can see it – then words will come. Every day people will look up and see, and face the memory of my grandson and how he lived and why he died. And every day they'll have to think things through and use words to say where they stand over and over.'

There were big clouds overhead. Ewan didn't remember seeing them so big since he was a boy when he and Sol Werbernuik had watched them sail by through the sky and named each one.

And so Ewan McCarthy undertook to build a boat in the fields above St Agnes, which he leased from the farmer who grazed cows there on condition that the cows still got to graze. He recruited Salazar to help him build the ark and together they have named it 'Good Hope' on the rising bow of the vessel. Its silhouette against the high trees and the sky can be seen from several vantage points down in the town. People drive past on the Padiham road and say, 'His poor wife, what must she think?' Some ask what the point of such a folly is and, in asking, discover a little about David Tallow and about his grandfather who built trawlers in Maine boat-yards and once had the mizen-mast snap two days out and saw two men die in the struggle to make for home but never saw his daughter born or knew that her own son died in such a way, though down in the town there are other men who keep their rifles cocked for fear the bear might reappear, not know-ing it to be safely stowed aboard the ark.

66 Slow Dancing

Ewan slow dances on the patio with Ann. The music comes from Tom who plays piano in the dining room with the patio doors slid back. Chrissie, heavily pregnant, sits in a wicker chair. She seems tired but she is fine. Her fingers stroke the leather of a battered baseball glove that lies in her lap.

'Why did you marry me?' Ewan asks.

'Because you were clever and serious and funny,' Ann says. 'And still a boy.'

'I thought I was very grown-up.'

'You couldn't fool me. I used to watch you sometimes wrestling with things. You always had to wrestle things to understand them. I never did. I was happy to let things wash past so long as there was you and the boys.'

'You think?'

'I believe that, yes. I was happy enough to be with you. You're not a woman, you wouldn't understand. I was happy to be here even when I was angry or sad at you.'

'And after all that push and pull I'm less sure of what I know now than when I set out.'

'Is that so bad?'

'Sometimes it seems so. Sometimes I think I don't know anything worth knowing for coming all this way. Things happening to me to bring me to this point have only served to push me away from what I thought I saw ahead, from what I wanted to be. And now I am beaten.'

'And now you are beaten,' she says.

Though in the way she slow dances with him, or in the words that she finds and whispers to him that even Chrissie sat close by and marvelling at them cannot hear, or in the way she looks at him, or rests her head against his evening shoulder, she says that for all the days that passed them by and delivered nothing, and those that made them sick and those that tired them, there are days of hope and surety and brotherhood. And those few days are the ones in the end that count when a life is reckoned in a random world.

Tom plays 'My Funny Valentine', a slow tune, not so sad, and Ewan dances with his wife close to him with the air cool on his arms, and what he feels for her seems less like the amphitheatre of angels he'd felt it had to be than some gas, some ether, inert and all around him that helps him breathe and carries the noise and burden of his life and is unseen unless he looks for it or unless it isn't there. And St Agnes as it always did gets on with life and will sometimes still be in some people's top ten, though not always for the Salazars and the Denny Arkins of this world, and here and there, depending on the day, there will be bell claps and markets, bears and saints and scoundrels and lost souls, and sadness, and hope, and resurrection.